I0661494

Charles Dickens

A Collection of Letters of Dickens, 1833-1870

Charles Dickens

A Collection of Letters of Dickens, 1833-1870

ISBN/EAN: 9783744763967

Printed in Europe, USA, Canada, Australia, Japan

Cover: Foto ©Andreas Hilbeck / pixelio.de

More available books at **www.hansebooks.com**

To. W. S. Martin from ✴✴✴ Christmas 1890

A Collection of

Letters of Dickens

A Collection of

Letters of Dickens

1833-1870

NEW YORK

Charles Scribner's Sons

1889

PUBLISHERS' NOTE.

The following Collection has been made from the three volumes of Dickens's letters edited by his sister-in-law and his eldest daughter, and published nearly a decade ago. The publishers believe that, valuable as the original edition must remain to many of Dickens's admirers, there is, at present, another audience for whom the letters will gain rather than lose by compression. It is needless to say that no word of the original has been changed, and that where omissions have been made they have, in every case—except that of entire letters—been indicated. In order to lose none of the interest of the volumes thus condensed, the work of selection has not been confined to complete letters, but has distinguished between the parts of each, in this way retaining, it is believed, everything essential in the first edition. Everything characteristic of the writer has especially been preserved—passages relating to his domestic relations, his love for his

children, his religious views, his opinions on pol-
itics and public questions generally, his personal
adventures, and every reference of any import to
his books or the characters they contain. And
thus, although many letters have been curtailed
and many others omitted, neither the color, hu-
mor, nor personal accent of the original three
volumes has suffered. The American allusions
have been nearly all retained. A few of the
notes are such as it has seemed advisable to add
to those of the original editors, whose explana-
tory "Narrative" has been dropped. The reader
will remark the necessary lack of chronological
continuity, but the chronological order has, of
course, been followed. The signature to the first
letter, which, though dateless, was written in 1835
—the days of Dickens's earliest authorship—is
given in fac-simile, as is one of the last letters
ever written by him.

Wednesday Eighth June 1870

My dear Sir

It would be quite inconceivable to me – but for your letter – that any reasonable reader could possibly attach a scriptural reference to a passage in a book of mine, reproducing a much abused social figure of speech, impressed into all sorts of service, on all sorts of inappropriate occasions, without the faintest connexion of it with its original source. I am truly shocked to find that any reader can make the mistake.

I have always striven in my
writings to express veneration for
the life and lessons of Our Saviour;
because I feel it; and because I
re-wrote that history for my
children — every one of whom
knew it from having it repeated
to them, long before they could

read, and almost as soon as they could speak.

But I have never made
proclamation of this from the house tops

Faithfully Yours

Charles Dickens

John M. Makeham Esqre

LETTERS

A COLLECTION OF

LETTERS OF DICKENS.

FURNIVAL'S INN, Wednesday Night, past 12.

Dear Henry :

I have just been ordered on a journey, the length of which is at present uncertain. I may be back on Sunday very probably, and start again on the following day. Should this be the case, you shall hear from me before.

Don't laugh. I am going (alone) in a gig ; and, to quote the eloquent inducement which the proprietors of Hampstead *chays* hold out to Sunday riders—"the gen'l'm'n drives himself." I am going into Essex and Suffolk. It strikes me I shall be spilt before I pay a turnpike. I have a presentiment I shall run over an only child before I reach Chelmsford, my first stage.

[1] Afterwards the husband of Dickens's second sister, Letitia.

Let the evident haste of this specimen of *The Polite Letter Writer* be its excuse, and

Believe me, dear Henry, most sincerely yours,

[TO MISS HOGARTH][1]

Sunday Evening.

*   *   *   *   *

I have at this moment got Pickwick and his friends on the Rochester coach, and they are going on swimmingly, in company with a very different character[2] from any I have yet described, who I flatter myself will make a decided hit. I want to get them from the ball to the inn before I go to bed; and I think that will take me until one or two o'clock at the earliest. The publishers will be here in the morning, so you will readily suppose I have no alternative but to stick at my desk.

*   *   *   *   *   *

[1] Afterwards Mrs. Dickens.
[2] Alfred Jingle.

[TO MASTER HASTINGS HUGHES]

DOUGHTY STREET, LONDON, Dec. 12th, 1838.

Respected Sir :

I have given Squeers one cut on the neck and two on the head, at which he appeared much surprised and began to cry, which, being a cowardly thing, is just what I should have expected from him—wouldn't you ?

I have carefully done what you told me in your letter about the lamb and the two " sheeps " for the little boys. They have also had some good ale and porter, and some wine. I am sorry you didn't say *what* wine you would like them to have. I gave them some sherry, which they liked very much, except one boy, who was a little sick and choked a good deal. He was rather greedy, and that's the truth, and I believe it went the wrong way, which I say served him right, and I hope you will say so too.

Nicholas had his roast lamb, as you said he was to, but he could not eat it all, and says if you do not mind his doing so he should like to have the rest hashed to-morrow with some greens, which he is very fond of, and so am I. He said he did not like to have his porter hot, for he thought it spoilt the flavour, so I let him have it cold. You should have seen him drink it. I thought he never would have left off. I also gave him three pounds of money, all in sixpences, to make it seem more, and he said directly that he should give more than half to his mamma and sister, and divide the rest with poor Smike. And I say he is a good fellow for saying so ; and if anybody says he isn't I am ready to fight him whenever they like—there !

Fanny Squeers shall be attended to, depend upon it. Your drawing of her is very like, except that I don't think the hair is quite curly enough. The nose is particularly like hers, and so are the legs. She is a nasty disagreeable thing, and I know it will make her very cross when she sees it; and what I say is that I hope it may. You will say the same I know—at least I think you will.

I meant to have written you a long letter, but I cannot write very fast when I like the person I am writing to, because that makes me think about them, and I like you, and so I tell you. Besides, it is just eight o'clock at night, and I always go to bed at eight o'clock, except when it is my birthday, and then I sit up to supper. So I will not say anything more besides this—and that is my love to you and Neptune ; and if you will drink my health every Christmas Day I will drink yours—come.

I am,

Respected Sir,

Your affectionate Friend.

P.S.—I don't write my name very plain, but you know what it is you know, so never mind.

[TO MR. W. C. MACREADY]

DOUGHTY STREET, Sunday.

My dear Macready :

I will have, if you please, three dozen of the extraordinary champagne ; and I am much obliged to you for recollecting me.

I ought not to be sorry to hear of your abdication,[1] but I am, notwithstanding, most heartily and sincerely sorry, for my own sake and the sake of thousands, who may now go and whistle for a theatre—at least, such a theatre as you gave them ; and I do now in my heart believe that for a long and dreary time that exquisite delight has passed away. If I may jest with my misfortunes, and quote the Portsmouth critic of Mr. Crummles's company, I say that : "As an exquisite embodiment of the poet's visions and a realization of human intellectuality, gilding with refulgent light our dreamy moments, and laying open a new and magic world before the mental eye, the drama is gone—perfectly gone."

With the same perverse and unaccountable feeling which causes a heart-broken man at a dear friend's funeral to see something irresistibly comical

---

[1] Of the management of Covent Garden Theatre.

in a red-nosed or one-eyed undertaker, I receive
your communication with ghostly facetiousness;
though on a moment's reflection I find better cause
for consolation in the hope that, relieved from your
most trying and painful duties, you will now have
leisure to return to pursuits more congenial to your
mind, and to move more easily and pleasantly among
your friends. In the long catalogue of the latter, I
believe that there is not one prouder of the name, or
more grateful for the store of delightful recollections
you have enabled him to heap up from boyhood,
than,

My dear Macready,
Yours always faithfully.

· [TO MR. GEORGE CATTERMOLE]

December 22d, 1840.

Dear George :

The child lying dead in the little sleeping-room,
which is behind the open screen. It is winter time,
so there are no flowers; but upon her breast and
pillow, and about her bed, there may be strips
of holly and berries, and such free green things.
Window overgrown with ivy. The little boy who
had that talk with her about angels may be by
the bedside, if you like it so; but I think it will be
quieter and more peaceful if she is quite alone. I
want it to express the most beautiful repose and

tranquillity, and to have something of a happy look, if death can.

2.

The child has been buried inside the church, and the old man, who cannot be made to understand that she is dead, repairs to the grave and sits there all day long, waiting for her arrival, to begin another journey. His staff and knapsack, her little bonnet and basket, etc., lie beside him. "She'll come to-morrow," he says when it gets dark, and goes sorrowfully home. I think an hour-glass running out would help the notion; perhaps her little things upon his knee, or in his hand.

I am breaking my heart over this story, and cannot bear to finish it.

Love to Missis.

Ever and always heartily.

[TO REV. WILLIAM HARNESS]

DEVONSHIRE TERRACE, Saturday Morning, Jan. 2d, 1841.

My dear Harness :

I should have been very glad to join your pleasant party, but all next week I shall be laid up with a broken heart, for I must occupy myself in finishing the *Curiosity Shop*, and it is such a painful task to me that I must concentrate myself upon it tooth and nail, and go out nowhere until it is done.

I have delayed answering your kind note in a vague hope of being heart-whole again by the seventh. The present state of my work, however (Christmas not being a very favourable season for making progress in such doings), assures me that this cannot be, and that I must heroically deny myself the pleasure you offer.

Always believe me,
Faithfully yours.

[TO MR. GEORGE CATTERMOLE]

Devonshire Terrace, Thursday, Jan. 14th, 1841.

My dear Cattermole :

I cannot tell you how much obliged I am to you for altering the child, or how much I hope that my wish in that respect didn't go greatly against the grain.

I saw the old inn this morning. Words cannot say how good it is. I can't bear the thought of its being cut, and should like to frame and glaze it in *statu quo* for ever and ever.

Will you do a little tail-piece for the *Curiosity* story?—only one figure if you like—giving some notion of the etherealised spirit of the child ; something like those little figures in the frontispiece. If

you will, and can despatch it at once, you will make
me happy.

I am, for the time being, nearly dead with work
and grief for the loss of my child.

Always, my dear George,
Heartily yours.

[TO MR. GEORGE CATTERMOLE]

DEVONSHIRE TERRACE, Thursday Night, Jan. 28th, 1841.

My dear George :

I sent to Chapman and Hall yesterday morning
about the second subject for No. 2 of *Barnaby,*
but found they had sent it to Browne.

The first subject of No. 3 I will either send to you
on Saturday, or, at latest, on Sunday morning. I
have also directed Chapman and Hall to send you
proofs of what has gone before, for reference, if you
need it.

I want to know whether you feel ravens in general and would fancy Barnaby's raven in particular.
Barnaby being an idiot, my notion is to have him
always in company with a pet raven, who is immeasurably more knowing than himself. To this end I
have been studying my bird, and think I could make
a very queer character of him. Should you like the
subject when this raven makes his first appearance ?

Faithfully always.

[TO MR. JOHN TOMLIN.][1]

I, DEVONSHIRE TERRACE, YORK GATE, REGENT'S PARK,
LONDON, Tuesday, Feb. 23d, 1841.

Dear Sir :

You are quite right in feeling assured that I
should answer the letter you have addressed to me.
If you had entertained a presentiment that it would
afford me sincere pleasure and delight to hear from
a warm-hearted and admiring reader of my books
in the backwoods of America, you would not have
been far wrong.

I thank you cordially and heartily both for your
letter and its kind and courteous terms. To think
that I have awakened a fellow-feeling and sympathy
with the creatures of many thoughtful hours among
the vast solitudes in which you dwell, is a source of
the purest delight and pride to me ; and believe me
that your expressions of affectionate remembrance
and approval, sounding from the green forests on the
banks of the Mississippi, sink deeper into my heart
and gratify it more than all the honorary distinc-
tions that all the courts in Europe could confer.

It is such things as these that make one hope one
does not live in vain, and that are the highest reward of an author's life. To be numbered among
the household gods of one's distant countrymen, and

[1] Published by Poe in 1842.

associated with their homes and quiet pleasures ; to be told that in each nook and corner of the world's great mass there lives one well-wisher who holds communion with one in the spirit, is a worthy fame indeed, and one which I would not barter for a mine of wealth.

That I may be happy enough to cheer some of your leisure hours for a very long time to come, and to hold a place in your pleasant thoughts is the earnest wish of " Boz."

And, with all good wishes for yourself, and with a sincere reciprocation of all your kindly feeling,

I am, dear Sir,

Faithfully yours.

[TO MR. R. MONCKTON MILNES]

DEVONSHIRE TERRACE, Wednesday, March 10th, 1841.

My dear Milnes :

I thank you very much for the *Nickleby* correspondence, which I will keep for a day or two, and return when I see you. Poor fellow! The long letter is quite admirable and most affecting.

I am not quite sure either of Friday or Saturday, for, independently of the *Clock* (which forever wants winding), I am getting a young brother off to New Zealand just now, and have my mornings sadly cut up in consequence. But, knowing your ways, I know I may say that I will come if I can ; and that if I can't I won't.

That Nellicide was the act of Heaven, as you may see any of these fine mornings when you look about you. If you knew the pain it gave me—but what am I talking of ? if you don't know, nobody does. I am glad to shake you by the hand again auto-graphically,

And am always,
Faithfully yours.

[TO MR. G. LOVEJOY]¹

DEVONSHIRE TERRACE, June 10th, 1841.

Dear Sir :

I am favoured with your note of yesterday's date, and lose no time in replying to it.

The sum you mention, though small I am aware in the abstract, is greater than I could afford for such a purpose ; as the mere sitting in the House and attending to my duties, if I were a member, would oblige me to make many pecuniary sacrifices, consequent upon the very nature of my pursuits.

The course you suggest did occur to me when I received your first letter, and I have very little doubt indeed that the Government would support me—perhaps to the whole extent. But I cannot satisfy myself that to enter Parliament under such circum-

---

¹ With regard to a proposal to represent Reading in Parliament.

stances would enable me to pursue that honourable
independence without which I could neither preserve my own respect nor that of my constituents.
I confess therefore (it may be from not having considered the points sufficiently, or in the right light)
that I cannot bring myself to propound the subject
to any member of the administration whom I know.
I am truly obliged to you, nevertheless, and am,

Dear Sir,

Faithfully yours.

[TO MR. WASHINGTON IRVING] [1]

My dear Sir :

There is no man in the world who could have
given me the heartfelt pleasure you have, by your
kind note of the 13th of last month. There is no
living writer, and there are very few among the
dead, whose approbation I should feel so proud to
earn. And with everything you have written upon
my shelves, and in my thoughts, and in my heart
of hearts, I may honestly and truly say so. If you
could know how earnestly I write this, you would
be glad to read it—as I hope you will be, faintly
guessing at the warmth of the hand I autobiograph-
ically hold out to you over the broad Atlantic.

---

[1] Published in *The Life and Letters of Washington Irving*, edited by
his nephew, Pierre M. Irving.

I wish I could find in j ⁓_ weicome letter some
ı cᶠ   ᴜᴜⱽention to visit England. I can't. I
have held it at arm's length, and taken a bird's- ᶺ
view of it, after reading it a great many tim⁓ , but
there is no greater encouragement in it this way
than on a microscopic ⁖ ₌ᴜtion. I should love to
go with you—⁓ 1 ᴜᴜve gone, God knows how often
—inᵗc Little Britain, and Eastcheap, and Green
Arbour Court, and Westminster Abbey. I should
like to travel with you, outside the last of the
coaches down to Bracebridge Hall. It would make
my heart glad to compare notes with you about that
shabby gentleman in the oilcloth hat and red nose,
who sat in the nine-cornered back-parlour of the Ma-
sons' Arms ; and about Robert Preston and the tal-
low-chandler's widow, whose sitting-room is second
nature to me ; and about all those delightful places
and people that I used to walk about and dream of
in the daytime, when a very small and not over-par-
ticularly-taken-care-of boy. I have a good deal to
say, too, about that dashing Alonzo de Ojeda, that
you can't help being fonder of than you ought to
be ; and much to hear concerning Moorish legend,
and poor unhappy Boabdil. Diedrich Knicker-
bocker I have worn to death in my pocket, and yet
I should show you his mutilated carcass with a joy
past all expression.

I have been so accustomed to associate you with

my pleasantest and happiest thoughts, and with my leisure hours, that I rush at once into full confidence with you, and fall, as it were naturally, and by the very laws of gravity, into your open arms. Questions come thronging to my pen as to the lips of people who meet after long hoping to do so. I don't know what to say first or what to leave unsaid, and am constantly disposed to break off and tell you again how glad I am this moment has arrived.

My dear Washington Irving, I cannot thank you enough for your cordial and generous praise, or tell you what deep and lasting gratification it has given me. I hope to have many letters from you, and to exchange a frequent correspondence. I send this to say so. After the first two or three I shall settle down into a connected style, and become gradually rational.

You know what the feeling is, after having written a letter, sealed it, and sent it off. I shall picture your reading this, and answering it before it has lain one night in the post-office. Ten to one that before the fastest packet could reach New York I shall be writing again.

Do you suppose the post-office clerks care to receive letters? I have my doubts. They get into a dreadful habit of indifference. A postman, I imagine, is quite callous. Conceive his delivering one to

2

himself, without being startled by a preliminary double knock !

Always your faithful Friend.

[TO MR. THOMAS MITTON]

TREMONT HOUSE, BOSTON, January 31st, 1842.

My dear Mitton :

  .   .   .   .   .   .

I can give you no conception of my welcome here. There never was a king or emperor upon the earth so cheered and followed by crowds, and entertained in public at splendid balls and dinners, and waited on by public bodies and deputations of all kinds. I have had one from the Far West—a journey of two thousand miles ! If I go out in a carriage, the crowd surround it and escort me home ; if I go to the theatre, the whole house (crowded to the door) rises as one man, and the timbers ring again. You cannot imagine what it is. I have five great public dinners on hand at this moment, and invitations from every town and village and city in the States.

There is a great deal afloat here in the way of subjects for description. I keep my eyes open pretty wide, and hope to have done so to some purpose by the time I come home.

  .   .   .   .   .   .

Always your faithful Friend.

[TO MR. WASHINGTON IRVING]

WASHINGTON, Monday Afternoon, March 21st, 1842.

My dear Irving :

We passed through—literally passed through—
this place again to-day. I did not come to see you,
for I really have not the heart to say "good-bye"
again, and felt more than I can tell you when we
shook hands last Wednesday.

You will not be at Baltimore, I fear? I thought,
at the time, that you only said you might be there,
to make our parting the gayer.

Wherever you go, God bless you! What pleasure
I have had in seeing and talking with you, I will
not attempt to say. I shall never forget it as long
as I live. What would I give, if we could have but
a quiet week together! Spain is a lazy place, and
its climate an indolent one. But if you have ever
leisure under its sunny skies to think of a man who
loves you, and holds communion with your spirit
oftener, perhaps, than any other person alive—leisure from listlessness, I mean—and will write to me
in London, you will give me an inexpressible amount
of pleasure.

Your affectionate friend.

[TO MR. W. C. MACREADY]

BALTIMORE, March 22d, 1842.

My dear Friend :

My dear Macready, I desire to be so honest and just to those who have so enthusiastically and earnestly welcomed me, that I burned the last letter I wrote to you—even to you to whom I would speak as to myself—rather than let it come with anything that might seem like an ill-considered word of disappointment. I preferred that you should think me neglectful (if you could imagine anything so wild) rather than I should do wrong in this respect. Still it is of no use. I *am* disappointed. This is not the republic I came to see ; this is not the republic of my imagination. I infinitely prefer a liberal monarchy—even with its sickening accompaniments of court circles—to such a government as this. The more I think of its youth and strength, the poorer and more trifling in a thousand aspects it appears in my eyes. In everything of which it has made a boast—excepting its education of the people and its care for poor children—it sinks immeasurably below the level I had placed it upon ; and England, even England, bad and faulty as the old land is, and miserable as millions of her people are, rises in the comparison.

You live here, Macready, as I have sometimes heard you imagining! *You!* Loving you with all my heart and soul, and knowing what your disposition really is, I would not condemn you to a year's residence on this side of the Atlantic for any money. Freedom of opinion! Where is it? I see a press more mean, and paltry, and silly, and disgraceful than any country I ever knew. If that is its standard, here it is. But I speak of Bancroft, and am advised to be silent on that subject, for he is "a black sheep—a Democrat." I speak of Bryant, and am entreated to be more careful, for the same reason. I speak of international copyright, and am implored not to ruin myself outright. I speak of Miss Martineau, and all parties—Slave Upholders and Abolitionists, Whigs, Tyler Whigs, and Democrats, shower down upon me a perfect cataract of abuse. "But what has she done? Surely she praised America enough!" "Yes, but she told us of some of our faults, and Americans can't bear to be told of their faults. Don't split on that rock, Mr. Dickens, don't write about America; we are so very suspicious."

Freedom of opinion! Macready, if I had been born here and had written my books in this country, producing them with no stamp of approval from any other land, it is my solemn belief that I should have lived and died poor, unnoticed, and a "black sheep" to boot. I never was more convinced of any-thing than I am of that.

The people are affectionate, generous, open-hearted, hospitable, enthusiastic, good-humoured, polite to women, frank and candid to all strangers, anxious to oblige, far less prejudiced than they have been described to be, frequently polished and re-fined, very seldom rude or disagreeable. I have made a great many friends here, even in public con-veyances, whom I have been truly sorry to part from. In the towns I have formed perfect attach-ments. I have seen none of that greediness and in-decorousness on which travellers have laid so much emphasis. I have returned frankness with frank-ness ; met questions not intended to be rude, with answers meant to be satisfactory : and have not spoken to one man, woman, or child of any degree, who has not grown positively affectionate before we parted. In the respects of not being left alone, and of being horribly disgusted by tobacco chewing and tobacco spittle, I have suffered considerably. The sight of slavery in Virginia, the hatred of British feeling upon the subject, and the miserable hints of the impotent indignation of the South, have pained me very much ; on the last head, of course, I have felt nothing but a mingled pity and amusement ; on the other, sheer distress. But however much I like the ingredients of this great dish, I cannot but come

back to the point at which I started, and say that
the dish itself goes against the grain with me, and
that I don't like it.

You know that I am truly a Liberal. I believe I
have as little pride as most men, and I am conscious
of not the smallest annoyance from being "hail
fellow well met" with everybody. I have not had
greater pleasure in the company of any set of men
among the thousands I have received (I hold a
regular levee every day, you know, which is duly
heralded and proclaimed in the newspapers) than in
that of the carmen of Hartford, who presented themselves in a body in their blue frocks, among a crowd
of well-dressed ladies and gentlemen, and bade me
welcome through their spokesman. They had all
read my books, and all perfectly understood them.
It is not these things I have in my mind when I say
that the man who comes to this country a Radical
and goes home again with his opinions unchanged,
must be a Radical on reason, sympathy, and reflection, and one who has so well considered the subject that he has no chance of wavering.

. . . . . .

As my pen is getting past its work, I have taken
a new one to say that

I am ever, my dear Macready,
Your faithful Friend.

BALTIMORE, UNITED STATES, March 22d, 1842.

My dear Friend :

We have been as far south as Richmond in Virginia (where they grow and manufacture tobacco,
and where the labour is all performed by slaves),
but the season in those latitudes is so intensely and
prematurely hot, that it was considered a matter of
doubtful expediency to go on to Charleston. For
this unexpected reason, and because the country between Richmond and Charleston is but a desolate
swamp the whole way, and because slavery is anything but a cheerful thing to live amidst, I have altered my route by the advice of Mr. Clay (the great
political leader in this country), and have returned
here previous to diving into the far West. We
start for that part of the country—which includes
mountain travelling, and lake travelling, and prairie
travelling—the day after to-morrow, at eight o'clock
in the morning ; and shall be in the West, and from
there going northward again, until the 30th of April
or 1st of May, when we shall halt for a week at
Niagara, before going further into Canada. We
have taken our passage home (God bless the word)
in the George Washington packet-ship from New
York. She sails on the 7th of June.

I have departed from my resolution not to accept

any more public entertainments; they have been proposed in every town I have visited—in favour of the people of St. Louis, my utmost western point. That town is on the borders of the Indian territory, a trifling distance from this place—only two thousand miles! At my second halting-place I shall be able to write to fix the day; I suppose it will be somewhere about the 12th of April. Think of my going so far towards the setting sun to dinner!

In every town where we stay, though it be only for a day, we hold a regular levee or drawing-room, where I shake hands on an average with five or six hundred people, who pass on from me to Kate, and are shaken again by her. Maclise's picture of our darlings stands upon a table or sideboard the while; and my travelling secretary, assisted very often by a committee belonging to the place, presents the people in due form. Think of two hours of this every day, and the people coming in by hundreds, all fresh, and piping hot, and full of questions, when we are literally exhausted and can hardly stand. I really do believe that if I had not a lady with me, I should have been obliged to leave the country and go back to England. But for her they never would leave me alone by day or night, and as it is, a slave comes to me now and then in the middle of the night with a letter, and waits at the bedroom door for an answer.

It was so hot at Richmond that we could scarcely breathe, and the peach and other fruit trees were in full blossom; it was so cold at Washington next day that we were shivering; but even in the same town you might often wear nothing but a shirt and trousers in the morning, and two greatcoats at night, the thermometer very frequently taking a little trip of thirty degrees between sunrise and sunset.

.   .   .   .   .   .

We were at the President's drawing-room while we were in Washington. I had a private audience besides, and was asked to dinner, but couldn't stay.

Parties—parties—parties—of course, every day and night. But it's not all parties. I go into the prisons, the police-offices, the watch-houses, the hospitals, the work-houses. I was out half the night in New York with two of their most famous constables; started at midnight, and went into every brothel, thieves' house, murdering hovel, sailor's dancing-place, and abode of villainy, both black and white, in the town. I went *incog.* behind the scenes to the little theatre where Mitchell is making a fortune. He has been rearing a little dog for me, and has called him "Boz." I am going to bring him home. In a word I go everywhere, and a hard life it is. But I am careful to drink hardly anything, and not to smoke at all. I have recourse to my medicine-chest whenever I feel at all bilious, and am, thank God, thoroughly well.

When I next write you, I shall have begun, I hope, to turn my face homeward. I have a great store of oddity and whimsicality, and am going now into the oddest and most characteristic part of this most queer country.

Always direct to the care of David Colden, Esq., 28, Laight Street, Hudson Square, New York. I received your Caledonia letter with the greatest joy.

Kate sends her best remembrances.

And I am always.

[TO MR. HENRY AUSTIN]

NIAGARA FALLS (English Side), Sunday, May 1st, 1842.

My dear Henry :

.   .   .   .   .   .

Is it not a horrible thing that scoundrel book-sellers should grow rich here from publishing books, the authors of which do not reap one farthing from their issue by scores of thousands ; and that every vile blackguard and detestable newspaper, so filthy and bestial that no honest man would admit one into his house for a scullery door-mat, should be able to publish those same writings side by side, cheek by jowl, with the coarsest and most obscene companions with which they must become con-

nected, in course of time, in people's minds? Is it
tolerable that besides being robbed and rifled an
author should be forced to appear in any form, in
any vulgar dress, in any atrocious company; that
he should have no choice of his audience, no con-
trol over his own distorted text, and that he should
be compelled to jostle out of the course the best
men in this country who only ask to live by writing? I vow before high heaven that my blood so
boils at these enormities, that when I speak about
them I seem to grow twenty feet high, and to swell
out in proportion. "Robbers that ye are," I think
to myself when I get upon my legs, "here goes!"

The places we have lodged in, the roads we have
gone over, the company we have been among, the
tobacco-spittle we have wallowed in, the strange cus-
toms we have complied with, the packing-cases in
which we have travelled, the woods, swamps, rivers,
prairies, lakes, and mountains we have crossed, are
all subjects for legends and tales at home; quires,
reams, wouldn't hold them.

    .   .   .   .   .   .

We purpose leaving this on Wednesday morning.
Give my love to Letitia and to mother, and always
believe me, my dear Henry,

                        Affectionately yours.

[TO MR. THOMAS LONGMAN]

ATHENÆUM, Friday Afternoon.

My dear Sir :

If I could possibly have attended the meeting yesterday I would most gladly have done so. But I have been up the whole night, and was too much exhausted even to write and say so before the proceedings came on.

I have fought the fight across the Atlantic with the utmost energy I could command ; have never been turned aside by any consideration for an instant ; am fresher for the fray than ever ; will battle it to the death, and die game to the last.

I am happy to say that my boy is quite well again. From being in perfect health he fell into alarming convulsions with the surprise and joy of our return.

I beg my regards to Mrs. Longman,

And am always,

Faithfully yours.

[TO MISS PARDOE]

DEVONSHIRE TERRACE, YORK GATE, REGENT'S PARK, July 19th, 1842.

Dear Madam :

I beg to set you right on one point in reference to the American robbers, which perhaps you do not quite understand.

The existing law allows them to reprint any English book, without any communication whatever with the author or anybody else. My books have all been reprinted on these agreeable terms.

But sometimes, when expectation is awakened there about a book before its publication, one firm of pirates will pay a trifle to procure early proofs of it, and get so much the start of the rest as they can obtain by the time necessarily consumed in printing it. Directly it is printed it is common property, and may be reprinted a thousand times. My circular only referred to such bargains as these.

I should add that I have no hope of the States doing justice in this dishonest respect, and therefore do not expect to overtake these fellows, but we may cry "Stop thief!" nevertheless, especially as they wince and smart under it.

Faithfully yours always.

[TO MRS. TROLLOPE]

1, DEVONSHIRE TERRACE, YORK GATE, REGENT'S PARK,
December 16th, 1842.

My dear Mrs. Trollope :

Let me thank you most cordially for your kind note, in reference to my *Notes*, which has given me true pleasure and gratification.

As I never scrupled to say in America, so I can have no delicacy in saying to you, that, allowing for

the change you worked in many social features of
American society, and for the time that has passed
since you wrote of the country, I am convinced that
there is no writer who has so well and accurately (I
need not add so entertainingly) described it, in many
of its aspects, as you have done ; and this renders
your praise the more valuable to me. I do not recollect ever to have heard or seen the charge of ex-
aggeration made against a feeble performance, though
in its feebleness, it may have been most untrue. It
seems to me essentially natural, and quite inevitable,
that common observers should accuse an uncommon
one of this fault, and I have no doubt that you were
long ago of this opinion ; very much to your own
comfort.

Mrs. Dickens begs me to thank you for your kind
remembrance of her, and to convey to you her best
regards. Always believe me,

Faithfully yours.

[TO PROFESSOR FELTON]

1, Devonshire Terrace, York Gate, Regent's Park,
London, 31st December, 1842.

My dear Felton :

Many and many happy New Years to you and
yours ! As many happy children as may be quite
convenient (no more !), and as many happy meetings
between them and our children, and between you

and us, as the kind fates in their utmost kindness shall favourably decree !

The American book (to begin with that) has been a most complete and thorough-going success. Four large editions have now been sold *and paid for*, and it has won golden opinions from all sorts of men, except our friend in F——, who is a miserable creature ; a disappointed man in great poverty, to whom I have ever been most kind and considerate (I need scarcely say that) ; and another friend in B——, no less a person than an illustrious gentleman named ——, who wrote a story called——. They have done no harm, and have fallen short of their mark, which, of course, was to annoy me. Now I am perfectly free from any diseased curiosity in such respects, and whenever I hear of a notice of this kind, I never read it ; whereby I always conceive (don't you ?) that I get the victory. With regard to your slave-owners, they may cry, till they are as black in the face as their own slaves, that Dickens lies. Dickens does not write for their satisfaction, and Dickens will not explain for their comfort. Dickens has the name and date of every newspaper in which every one of those advertisements appeared, as they know perfectly well ; but Dickens does not choose to give them, and will not at any time between this and the day of judgment. . . .

I have been hard at work on my new book, of

which the first number has just appeared. The Paul
Joneses who pursue happiness and profit at other
men's cost will no doubt enable you to read it, almost
as soon as you receive this. I hope you will like it.
And I particularly commend, my dear Felton, one
Mr. Pecksniff and his daughters to your tender regards. I have a kind of liking for them myself.

Blessed star of morning, such a trip as we had
into Cornwall, just after Longfellow went away!
The "we" means Forster, Maclise, Stanfield (the
renowned marine painter), and the Inimitable Boz.
We went down into Devonshire by the railroad, and
there we hired an open carriage from an innkeeper,
patriotic in all Pickwick matters, and went on with
post-horses. Sometimes we travelled all night,
sometimes all day, sometimes both. I kept the
joint-stock purse, ordered all the dinners, paid all
the turnpikes, conducted facetious conversations
with the post-boys, and regulated the pace at which
we travelled. Stanfield (an old sailor) consulted an
enormous map on all disputed points of wayfaring ;
and referred, moreover, to a pocket-compass and
other scientific instruments. The luggage was in
Forster's department ; and Maclise, having nothing
particular to do, sang songs. Heavens! If you
could have seen the necks of bottles—distracting
in their immense varieties of shape—peering out of
the carriage pockets ! If you could have witnessed

8

the deep devotion of the post-boys, the wild attachment of the hostlers, the maniac glee of the waiters !
If you could have followed us into the earthy old
churches we visited, and into the strange caverns
on the gloomy sea-shore, and down into the depths
of mines, and up to the tops of giddy heights where
the unspeakably green water was roaring, I don't
know how many hundred feet below ! If you could
have seen but one gleam of the bright fires by which
we sat in the big rooms of ancient inns at night,
until long after the small hours had come and gone,
or smelt but one steam of the hot punch (not white,
dear Felton, like that amazing compound I sent you
a taste of, but a rich, genial, glowing brown) which
came in every evening in a huge brown china bowl !
I never laughed in my life as I did on this journey.
It would have done you good to hear me. I was
choking and gasping and bursting the buckle off
the back of my stock, all the way. And Stanfield
(who is very much of your figure and temperament,
but fifteen years older) got into such apoplectic en-
tanglements that we were often obliged to beat him
on the back with portmanteaus before we could
recover him. Seriously, I do believe there never
was such a trip. And they made such sketches,
those two men, in the most romantic of our halt-
ing-places, that you would have sworn we had the
Spirit of Beauty with us, as well as the Spirit of

Fun. But stop till you come to England—I say no more.

The actuary of the national debt couldn't calculate the number of children who are coming here on Twelfth Night, in honour of Charley's birthday, for which occasion I have provided a magic lantern and divers other tremendous engines of that nature. But the best of it is that Forster and I have purchased between us the entire stock-in-trade of a conjurer, the practice and display whereof is intrusted to me. And O my dear eyes, Felton, if you could see me conjuring the company's watches into impossible tea-caddies, and causing pieces of money to fly, and burning pocket-handkerchiefs without hurting 'em, and practising in my own room, without anybody to admire, you would never forget it as long as you live. In those tricks which require a confederate, I am assisted (by reason of his imperturbable good humour) by Stanfield, who always does his part exactly the wrong way, to the unspeakable delight of all beholders. We come out on a small scale, to-night, at Forster's, where we see the old year out and the new one in. Particulars shall be forwarded in my next.

I have quite made up my mind that F—— really believes he *does* know you personally, and has all his life. He talks to me about you with such gravity that I am afraid to grin, and feel it necessary to look quite serious. Sometimes he *tells* me things about you, doesn't ask me, you know, so that I am occasionally perplexed beyond all telling, and begin to think it was he, and not I, who went to America. It's the queerest thing in the world.

The book I was to have given Longfellow for you is not worth sending by itself, being only a Barnaby. But I will look up some manuscript for you (I think I have that of the *American Notes* complete), and will try to make the parcel better worth its long conveyance. With regard to Maclise's pictures, you certainly are quite right in your impression of them ; but he is " such a discursive devil " (as he says about himself), and flies off at such odd tangents, that I feel it difficult to convey to you any general notion of his purpose. I will try to do so when I write again. I want very much to know about —— and that charming girl. . . . Give me full particulars. Will you remember me cordially to Sumner, and say I thank him for his welcome letter? The like to Hillard, with many regards to himself and his wife, with whom I had one night a little conversation which I shall not readily forget. The like to Washington Allston, and all friends who care for me and have outlived my book. . . . Always, my dear Felton,

   With true regard and affection, yours.

1, DEVONSHIRE TERRACE, YORK GATE, REGENT'S PARK,
LONDON, March 2d, 1843.

My dear Felton :
I don't know where to begin, but plunge head-
long with a terrible splash into this letter, on the
chance of turning up somewhere.

Hurrah! Up like a cork again, with *The North
American Review* in my hand. Like you, my dear
——, and I can say no more in praise of it, though
I go on to the end of the sheet. You cannot think
how much notice it has attracted here. Brougham
called the other day, with the number (thinking I
might not have seen it), and I being out at the time,
he left a note speaking of it, and of the writer, in
terms that warmed my heart. Lord Ashburton (one
of whose people wrote a notice in the *Edinburgh*
which they have since publicly contradicted) also
wrote to me about it in just the same strain. And
many others have done the like.

I am in great health and spirits and powdering
away at *Chuzzlewit*, with all manner of facetiousness rising up before me as I go on. . . . On
the 4th of April I am going to preside at a public
dinner for the benefit of the printers ; and if you
were a guest at that table, wouldn't I smite you on
the shoulder, harder than ever I rapped the well-

beloved back of Washington Irving at the City
Hotel in New York!

You were asking me—I love to say asking, as if
we could talk together—about Maclise. He is such
a discursive fellow, and so eccentric in his might,
that on a mental review of his pictures I can hardly
tell you of them as leading to any one strong purpose. But the annual Exhibition of the Royal
Academy comes off in May, and then I will endeavour to give you some notion of him. He is a
tremendous creature, and might do anything. But,
like all tremendous creatures, he takes his own way,
and flies off at unexpected breaches in the conventional wall.

    .   .   .   .   .   .

      Faithfully always, my dear Felton.

[TO MR. DAVID DICKSON]

1, DEVONSHIRE TERRACE, YORK GATE, REGENT'S PARK,
May 10th, 1843.

Sir :

Permit me to say, in reply to your letter, that
you do not understand the intention (I dare say
the fault is mine) of that passage in the *Pickwick
Papers* which has given you offence. The design
of "the Shepherd" and of this and every other allu-
sion to him is, to show how sacred things are degraded, vulgarized, and rendered absurd when per-

sons who are utterly incompetent to teach the commonest things take upon themselves to expound such mysteries, and how, in making mere cant phrases of divine words, these persons miss the spirit in which they had their origin. I have seen a great deal of this sort of thing in many parts of England, and I never knew it lead to charity or good deeds.

Whether the great Creator of the world and the creature of his hands, moulded in his own image, be quite so opposite in character as you believe, is a question which it would profit us little to discuss. I like the frankness and candour of your letter and thank you for it. That every man who seeks heaven must be born again, in good thoughts of his Maker, I sincerely believe. That it is expedient for every hound to say so in a certain snuffling form of words, to which he attaches no good meaning, I do not believe. I take it there is no difference between us.

Faithfully yours.

[TO PROFESSOR FELTON]

BROADSTAIRS, KENT, September 1st, 1843.

My dear Felton :
    If I thought it in the nature of things that you and I could ever agree on paper, touching a certain Chuzzlewitian question whereupon F—— tells me

you have remarks to make, I should immediately walk into the same tooth and nail. But as I don't, I won't. Contenting myself with this prediction, that one of these years and days, you will write or say to me : " My dear Dickens, you were right, though rough, and did a world of good, though you got most thoroughly hated for it." To which I shall reply : " My dear Felton, I looked a long way off and not immediately under my nose." . . . At which sentiment you will laugh, and I shall laugh ; and then (for I foresee this will all happen in my land) we shall call for another pot of porter and two or three dozen of oysters.

Now, don't you in your own heart and soul quarrel with me for this long silence? Not half so much as I quarrel with myself, I know ; but if you could read half the letters I write to you in imagination, you would swear by me for the best of correspondents. The truth is, that when I have done my morning's work, down goes my pen, and from that minute I feel it a positive impossibility to take it up again, until imaginary butchers and bakers wave me to my desk. I walk about brimful of letters, facetious descriptions, touching morsels, and pathetic friend-ships, but can't for the soul of me uncork myself. The post-office is my rock ahead. My average number of letters that _must_ be written every day is, at the least, a dozen. And you could no more know what I was writing to you spiritually, from the perusal of the bodily thirteenth, than you could tell from my hat what was going on in my head, or could read my heart on the surface of my flannel waistcoat.

This is a little fishing-place ; intensely quiet ; built on a cliff, whereon—in the centre of a tiny semicircular bay—our house stands ; the sea rolling and dashing under the windows. Seven miles out are the Goodwin Sands (you've heard of the Goodwin Sands?) whence floating lights perpetually wink after dark, as if they were carrying on intrigues with the servants. Also there is a big lighthouse called the North Foreland on a hill behind the village, a severe parsonic light, which reproves the young and giddy floaters, and stares grimly out upon the sea. Under the cliff are rare good sands, where all the children assemble every morning and throw up impossible fortifications, which the sea throws down again at high water. Old gentlemen and ancient ladies flirt after their own manner in two reading-rooms and on a great many scattered seats in the open air. Other old gentlemen look all day through telescopes and never see anything. In a bay-window in a one-pair sits, from nine o'clock to one, a gentleman with rather long hair and no neckcloth, who writes and grins as if he thought he were very funny indeed. His name is Boz. At one he disappears, and presently emerges from a bathing-machine, and

may be seen—a kind of salmon-colored porpoise—
splashing about in the ocean.   After that he may be
seen in another bay-window on the ground-floor, eat-
ing a strong lunch ; after that, walking a dozen miles
or so, or lying on his back in the sand reading a
book.   Nobody bothers him unless they know he is
disposed to be talked to ; and I am told he is very
comfortable indeed.   He's as brown as a berry, and
they *do* say is a small fortune to the innkeeper who
sells beer and cold punch.   But this is mere rumour.
Sometimes he goes up to London (eighty miles, or
so, away), and then I'm told there is a sound in Lincoln's Inn Fields at night, as of men laughing, together with a clinking of knives and forks and wine-
glasses.

.   .   .   .   .   .

I very often dream I am in America again ; but,
strange to say, I never dream of you.   I am always
endeavouring to get home in disguise, and have a
dreary sense of the distance.   *À propos* of dreams,
is it not a strange thing if writers of fiction never
dream of their own creations ; recollecting, I suppose, even in their dreams, that they have no real
existence ?   *I* never dreamed of any of my own
characters, and I feel it so impossible that I would
wager Scott never did of his, real as they are.   I had
a good piece of absurdity in my head a night or two
ago.   I dreamed that somebody was dead.   I don't

know who, but it's not to the purpose. It was a
private gentleman, and a particular friend; and I
was greatly overcome when the news was broken
to me (very delicately) by a gentleman in a cocked
hat, top boots, and a sheet. Nothing else. "Good
God!" I said, "is he dead?" "He is as dead, sir,"
rejoined the gentleman, "as a door-nail. But we
must all die, Mr. Dickens, sooner or later, my dear
sir." "Ah!" I said. "Yes, to be sure. Very true.
But what did he die of?" The gentleman burst
into a flood of tears, and said, in a voice broken by
emotion : "He christened his youngest child, sir,
with a toasting-fork." I never in my life was so
affected as at his having fallen a victim to this complaint. It carried a conviction to my mind that he
never could have recovered. I knew that it was the
most interesting and fatal malady in the world; and
I wrung the gentleman's hand in a convulsion of
respectful admiration, for I felt that this explanation
did equal honour to his head and heart!

What do you think of Mrs. Gamp? And how do
you like the undertaker? I have a fancy that they
are in your way. Oh heaven! such green woods as I
was rambling among down in Yorkshire, when I was
getting that done last July! For days and weeks we
never saw the sky but through green boughs; and
all day long I cantered over such soft moss and turf,
that the horse's feet scarcely made a sound upon it.

We have some friends in that part of the country (close to Castle Howard, where Lord Morpeth's father dwells in state, *in* his park indeed), who are the jolliest of the jolly, keeping a big old country house, with an ale cellar something larger than a reasonable church, and everything, like Goldsmith's bear dances, "in a concatenation accordingly." Just the place for you, Felton! We performed some madnesses there in the way of forfeits, picnics, rustic games, inspections of ancient monasteries at midnight, when the moon was shining, that would have gone to your heart, and, as Mr. Weller says, "come out on the other side." . . .

Write soon, my dear Felton ; and if I write to you less often than I would, believe that my affectionate heart is with you always. Loves and regards to all friends, from yours ever and ever.

Very faithfully yours.

[TO PROFESSOR FELTON]

DEVONSHIRE TERRACE, LONDON, January 2d, 1844.

My very dear Felton :

You are a prophet, and had best retire from business straightway. Yesterday morning, New Year's Day, when I walked into my little workroom after breakfast, and was looking out of window at the snow in the garden—not seeing it particularly well in consequence of some staggering suggestions of last night, whereby I was beset—the postman came to the door with a knock, for which I denounced him from my heart. Seeing your hand upon the cover of a letter which he brought, I immediately blessed him, presented him with a glass of whisky, inquired after his family (they are all well), and opened the despatch with a moist and oystery twinkle in my eye. And on the very day from which the new year dates, I read your New Year congratulations as punctually as if you lived in the next house. Why don't you?

Now, if instantly on the receipt of this you will send a free and independent citizen down to the Cunard wharf at Boston, you will find that Captain Hewett, of the Britannia steamship (my ship), has a small parcel for Professor Felton of Cambridge ; and in that parcel you will find a *Christmas Carol* in prose ; being a short story of Christmas by Charles Dickens. Over which *Christmas Carol* Charles Dickens wept and laughed and wept again, and excited himself in a most extraordinary manner in the composition ; and thinking whereof he walked about the black streets of London, fifteen and twenty miles many a night when all the sober folks had gone to bed. . . . Its success is most prodigious. And by every post all manner of strangers write all manner of letters to him about their homes and hearths, and how this same Carol is read aloud there, and kept on a little shelf by itself. Indeed, it is the greatest success, as I am told, that this ruffian and rascal has ever achieved.

·   ·   ·   ·   ·   ·

I wrote to Prescott about his book, with which I was perfectly charmed. I think his descriptions masterly, his style brilliant, his purpose manly and gallant always. The introductory account of Aztec civilization impressed me exactly as it impressed you. From beginning to end the whole history is enchanting and full of genius. I only wonder that, having such an opportunity of illustrating the doctrine of visible judgments, he never remarks, when Cortes and his men tumble the idols down the temple steps and call upon the people to take notice that their gods are powerless to help themselves, that possibly if some intelligent native had tumbled down the image of the Virgin or patron saint after them nothing very remarkable might have ensued in consequence.

Of course you like Macready. Your name's Felton. I wish you could see him play Lear. It is stupendously terrible. But I suppose he would be slow to act it with the Boston company.

Hearty remembrances to Sumner, Longfellow, Prescott, and all whom you know I love to remem-

ber.   Countless happy years to you and yours, my
dear Felton, and some instalment of them, however
slight, in England, in the loving company of
          THE PROSCRIBED ONE.
               Oh, breathe not his name !

.

          [TO MR. DOUGLAS JERROLD]

          CREMONA, Saturday Night, October 16th, 1844.
My dear Jerrold :
     .   .   .   .   .   .
I have never in my life been so struck by any
place as by Venice.   It is *the* wonder of the world.
Dreamy, beautiful, inconsistent, impossible, wicked,
shadowy, d——able old place.   I entered it by
night, and the sensation of that night and the bright
morning that followed is a part of me for the rest
of my existence.   And, oh God! the cells below the
water, underneath the Bridge of Sighs ; the nook
where the monk came at midnight to confess the
political offender ; the bench where he was stran-
gled ; the deadly little vault in which they tied him
in a sack, and the stealthy crouching little door
through which they hurried him into a boat, and
bore him away to sink him where no fisherman dare
cast his net—all shown by torches that blink and
wink, as if they were ashamed to look upon the
gloomy theatre of sad horrors ; past and gone as

they are, these things stir a man's blood, like a
great wrong or passion of the instant. And with
these in their minds, and with a museum there,
having a chamber full of such frightful instruments
of torture as the devil in a brain fever could scarcely
invent, there are hundreds of parrots, who will de-
claim to you in speech and print, by the hour together, on the degeneracy of the times in which a
railroad is building across the water at Venice ;
instead of going down on their knees, the drivellers,
and thanking Heaven that they live in a time when
iron makes roads, instead of prison bars and engines
for driving screws into the skulls of innocent men.
Before God, I could almost turn bloody-minded,
and shoot the parrots of our island with as little
compunction as Robinson Crusoe shot the parrots
in his.

.   .   .   .   .   .

Always your Friend and Admirer.

[TO MRS. CHARLES DICKENS]

PARMA, ALBERGO DELLA POSTA, Friday, Nov. 8th, 1844.

My dearest Kate :

"If missis could see us to-night, what would she
say ?" That was the brave C.'s remark last night
at midnight, and he had reason. We left Genoa, as
you know, soon after five on the evening of my de-

parture; and in company with the lady whom you
saw, and the dog whom I don't think you did see,
travelled all night at the rate of four miles an hour
over bad roads, without the least refreshment until
daybreak, when the brave and myself escaped into a
miserable caffè while they were changing horses, and
got a cup of that drink hot. That same day, a few
hours afterwards, between ten and eleven, we came
to (I hope) the d——dest inn in the world, where,
in a vast chamber, rendered still more desolate by
the presence of a most offensive specimen of what
D'Israeli calls the Mosaic Arab (who had a beautiful
girl with him), I regaled upon a breakfast, almost as
cold, and damp, and cheerless, as myself. Then, in
another coach, much smaller than a small Fly, I was
packed up with an old padre, a young Jesuit, a pro-
vincial avvocato, a private gentleman with a very red
nose and a very wet brown umbrella, and the brave
C. and I went on again at the same pace through
the mud and rain until four in the afternoon, when
there was a place in the coupé (two indeed), which
I took, holding that select compartment in company
with a very ugly but very agreeable Tuscan "gent,"
who said "*gia*" instead of "*si*," and rung some
other changes in this changing language, but with
whom I got on very well, being extremely conver-
sational. We were bound, as you know perhaps,
for Piacenza, but it was discovered that we couldn't

4

get to Piacenza, and about ten o'clock at night we
halted at a place called Stradella, where the inn was
a series of queer galleries open to the night, with a
great courtyard full of wagons and horses, and "*ve-
lociferi*," and what not in the centre. It was bitter
cold and very wet, and we all walked into a bare
room (mine !) with two immensely broad beds on
two deal dining-tables, a third great empty table,
the usual washing-stand tripod, with a slop-basin on
it, and two chairs. And then we walked up and
down for three-quarters of an hour or so, while dinner, or supper, or whatever it was, was getting
ready. This was set forth (by way of variety) in the
old priest's bedroom, which had two more immensely
broad beds on two more deal dining-tables in it.
The first dish was a cabbage boiled in a great quantity of rice and hot water, the whole flavoured with
cheese. I was so cold that I thought it comfortable, and so hungry that a bit of cabbage, when I
found such a thing floating my way, charmed me.
After that we had a dish of very little pieces of pork,
fried with pigs' kidneys ; after that a fowl ; after
that something very red and stringy, which I think
was veal ; and after that two tiny little new-born-
baby-looking turkeys, very red and very swollen.
Fruit, of course, to wind up, and garlic in one shape
or another in every course. I made three jokes at
supper (to the immense delight of the company),

and retired early. The brave brought in a bush or two and made a fire, and after that a glass of screeching hot brandy and water ; that bottle of his being full of brandy. I drank it at my leisure, undressed before the fire, and went into one of the beds. The brave reappeared about an hour afterwards and went into the other ; previously tying a pocket-handkerchief round and round his head in a strange fashion, and giving utterance to the sentiment with which this letter begins. At five this morning we resumed our journey, still through mud and rain, and at about eleven arrived at Piacenza; where we fellow-passengers took leave of one another in the most affectionate manner. As there was no coach on till six at night, and as it was a very grim, despondent sort of place, and as I had had enough of diligences for one while, I posted forward here in the strangest carriages ever beheld, which we changed when we changed horses. We arrived here before six. The hotel is quite French. I have dined very well in my own room on the second floor ; and it has two beds in it, screened off from the room by drapery. I only use one to-night, and that is already made. I purpose posting on to Bologna, if I can arrange it, at twelve to-morrow; seeing the sights here first. It is dull work this travelling alone. My only comfort is in motion.

.   .   .   .   .   .

Give my best love to Georgy, and my paternal
blessing to
> Mamey,
> Katey,
> Charley,
> Wally,
>   and
> Chickenstalker.

P.S.—Get things in their places. I can't bear to
picture them otherwise.

P.P.S.—I think I saw Roche sleeping with his
head on the lady's shoulder, in the coach. I couldn't
swear it, and the light was deceptive But I think
I did.
Alla sign*
    Sign* Dickens.
Palazzo Peschiere, Genova.

[TO MR. W. C. MACREADY]

HÔTEL BRISTOL, PARIS, Thursday Night,
Nov. 28th, 1844, Half-past Ten.

My dearest Macready :
Since I wrote to you what would be called in law
proceedings the exhibit marked A, I have been
round to the Hôtel Brighton, and personally examined and cross-examined the attendants. It is pain-

fully clear to me that I shall not see you to-night, nor until Tuesday, the 10th of December, when, please God, I shall re-arrive here, on my way to my Italian bowers. I mean to stay all the Wednesday and all the Thursday in Paris. One night to see you act (my old delight when you little thought of such a being in existence), and one night to read to you and Mrs. Macready (if that scamp of Lincoln's Inn Fields has not anticipated me) my little Christmas book,[1] in which I have endeavoured to plant an indignant right-hander on the eye of certain wicked Cant that makes my blood boil, which I hope will not only cloud that eye with black and blue, but many a gentle one with crystal of the finest sort. God forgive me, but I think there are good things in the little story !

.   .   .   .   .   .

[TO MRS. CHARLES DICKENS]

PIAZZA COFFEE HOUSE, COVENT GARDEN,
Monday, Dec. 2d, 1844.

My dearest Kate :

.   .   .   .

The little book is now, as far as I am concerned, all ready. One cut of Doyle's and one of Leech's I found so unlike my ideas, that I had them both to breakfast with me this morning, and with that win-

[1] *The Chimes.*

ning manner which you know of, got them with the highest good humour to do both afresh. They are now hard at it. Stanfield's readiness, delight, wonder at my being pleased with what he has done is delicious. Mac's frontispiece is charming. The book is quite splendid ; the expenses will be very great, I have no doubt.

Anybody who has heard it has been moved in the most extraordinary manner. Forster read it (for dramatic purposes) to A'Beckett. He cried so much and so painfully, that Forster didn't know whether to go on or stop ; and he called next day to say that any expression of his feeling was beyond his power. But that he believed it, and felt it to be—I won't say what.

As the reading comes off to-morrow night, I had better not despatch my letters to you until *Wednesday's* post. I must close to save this (heartily tired I am, and I dine at Gore House to-day), so with love to Georgy, Mamey, Katey, Charley, Wally, and Chickenstalker, ever, believe me,

Yours, with true affection.

P.S.—If you had seen Macready last night, undisguisedly sobbing and crying on the sofa as I read, you would have felt, as I did, what a thing it is to have power.

1, DEVONSHIRE TERRACE, July 28th, 1845.

My dear Sir :

As my note is to bear reference to business, I will make it as short and plain as I can. I think I could write a pretty good and a well-timed article on the *Punishment of Death*, and sympathy with great criminals, instancing the gross and depraved curiosity that exists in reference to them, by some of the outrageous things that were written, done, and said in recent cases. But as I am not sure that my views would be yours, and as their statement would be quite inseparable from such a paper, I will briefly set down their purport that you may decide for yourself.

Society, having arrived at that state in which it spares bodily torture to the worst criminals, and having agreed, if criminals be put to death at all, to kill them in the speediest way, I consider the question with reference to society, and not at all with reference to the criminal, holding that, in a case of cruel and deliberate murder, he is already mercifully and sparingly treated. But, as a question for the deliberate consideration of all reflective persons, I put

[1] Published in *Selection from the Correspondence of the late Macvey Napier, Esq.*, editor of *The Edinburgh Review*, edited by his son, Macvey Napier.

this view of the case. With such very repulsive and
odious details before us, may it not be well to inquire whether the punishment of death be beneficial
to society? I believe it to have a horrible fascination for many of those persons who render themselves liable to it, impelling them onward to the ac-
quisition of a frightful notoriety; and (setting aside
the strong confirmation of this idea afforded in individual instances) I presume this to be the case in
very badly regulated minds, when I observe the
strange fascination which everything connected with
this punishment, or the object of it, possesses for
tens of thousands of decent, virtuous, well-conducted
people, who are quite unable to resist the published
portraits, letters, anecdotes, smilings, snuff-takings,
of the bloodiest and most unnatural scoundrel with
the gallows before him. I observe that this strange
interest does not prevail to anything like the same
degree where death is not the penalty. Therefore
I connect it with the dread and mystery surrounding
death in any shape, but especially in this avenging
form, and am disposed to come to the conclusion
that it produces crime in the criminally disposed,
and engenders a diseased sympathy—morbid and
bad, but natural and often irresistible—among the
well conducted and gentle. Regarding it as doing
harm to both these classes, it may even then be right
to inquire, whether it has any salutary influence on

those small knots and specks of people, mere bubbles in the living ocean, who actually behold its infliction with their proper eyes. On this head it is scarcely possible to entertain a doubt, for we know that robbery, and obscenity, and callous indifference are of no commoner occurrence anywhere than at the foot of the scaffold. Furthermore, we know that all exhibitions of agony and death have a tendency to brutalise and harden the feelings of men, and have always been the most rife among the fiercest people. Again, it is a great question whether ignorant and dissolute persons (ever the great body of spectators, as few others will attend), seeing *that* murder done, and not having seen the other, will not, almost of necessity, sympathise with the man who dies before them, especially as he is shown, a martyr to their fancy, tied and bound, alone among scores, with every kind of odds against him.

I should take all these threads up at the end by a vivid little sketch of the origin and progress of such a crime as Hocker's, stating a somewhat parallel case, but an imaginary one, pursuing its hero to his death, and showing what enormous harm he does *after* the crime for which he suffers. I should state none of these positions in a positive sledge-hammer way, but tempt and lure the reader into the discussion of them in his own mind ; and so we come to this at last—whether it be for the benefit of society to ele-

vate even this crime to the awful dignity and notoriety of death ; and whether it would not be much
more to its advantage to substitute a mean and
shameful punishment, degrading the deed and the
committer of the deed, and leaving the general com-
passion to expend itself upon the only theme at
present quite forgotten in the history, that is to say,
the murdered person.

I do not give you this as an outline of the paper,
which I think I could make attractive. It is merely
an exposition of the inferences to which its whole
philosophy must tend.

Always faithfully yours.

[TO MR. W. H. WILLS]

DEVONSHIRE TERRACE, March 4th, 1846.

My dear Mr. Wills :

.   .   .   .   .   .

Tell Powell (with my regards) that he needn't
"deal with" the American notices of the *Cricket*.
I never read one word of their abuse, and I should
think it base to read their praises. It is something
to know that one is righted so soon ; and knowing
that, I can afford to know no more.

Ever faithfully yours.

GENEVA, Saturday, October 24th, 1846.

My dear Macready :

The welcome sight of your handwriting moves me (though I have nothing to say) to show you mine, and if I could recollect the passage in *Virginius* I would paraphase it, and say, " Does it seem to tremble, boy ? Is it a loving autograph ? Does it beam with friendship and affection ? " all of which I say, as I write, with—oh Heaven !—such a splendid imitation of you, and finally give you one of those grasps and shakes with which I have seen you make the young Icilius stagger again.

Here I am, running away from a bad headache as Tristram Shandy ran away from death, and lodging for a week in the Hôtel de l'Écu de Genève, wherein there is a large mirror shattered by a cannon-ball in the late revolution. A revolution, whatever its merits, achieved by free spirits, nobly generous and moderate, even in the first transports of victory, elevated by a splendid popular education, and bent on freedom from all tyrants, whether their crowns be shaven or golden. The newspapers may tell you what they please. I believe there is no country on earth but Switzerland in which a violent change could have been effected in the Christian spirit shown in this place, or in the same proud, independent, gallant style. Not one halfpennyworth of property was lost, stolen, or strayed. Not one atom of party malice survived the smoke of the last gun. Nothing is expressed in the Government addresses to the citizens but a regard for the general happiness, and injunctions to forget all animosities ; which they are practically obeying at every turn, though the late Government (of whose spirit I had some previous knowledge) did load the guns with such material as should occasion gangrene in the wounds, and though the wounded *do* die, consequently, every day, in the hospital, of sores that in themselves were nothing.

.   .   .   .   .   .

It is a great pleasure to me, my dear Macready, to hear from yourself, as I had previously heard from Forster, that you are so well pleased with *Dombey*, which is evidently a great success and a great hit, thank God ! I felt that Mrs. Brown was strong, but I was not at all afraid of giving as heavy a blow as I could to a piece of hot iron that lay ready at my hand. For that is my principle always, and I hope to come down with some heavier sledge-hammers than that.

.   .   .   .   .   .

Kate and Georgy send their best loves to Mrs. and Miss Macready, and all your house.

                    Your most affectionate Friend.

[TO MR. WALTER SAVAGE LANDOR]

PARIS, Sunday, November 22d, 1846.

Young Man :

I will not go there if I can help it. I have not
the least confidence in the value of your introduction
to the Devil. I can't help thinking that it would be
of better use "the other way, the other way," but I
won't try it there, either, at present, if I can help it.
Your godson says, is that your duty? and he begs
me to enclose a blush newly blushed for you.

.   .   .   .   .   .

Don't be hard upon the Swiss. They are a thorn
in the sides of European despots, and a good wholesome people to live near Jesuit-ridden kings on the
brighter side of the mountains. My hat shall ever
be ready to be thrown up, and my glove ever ready
to be thrown down for Switzerland. If you were the
man I took you for, when I took you (as a godfather)
for better and for worse, you would come to Paris
and amaze the weak walls of the house I haven't
found with that steady snore of yours, which I once
heard piercing the door of your bedroom in Devonshire Terrace, reverberating along the bell-wire in
the hall, so getting outside into the street, playing
Eolian harps among the area railings, and going
down the New Road like the blast of a trumpet.

I forgive you your reviling of me : there's a shov-
elful of live coals for your head—does it burn? And
am, with true affection—does it burn now ?—

Ever yours.

[TO REV. EDWARD TAGART]

PARIS, 48, RUE DE COURCELLES, ST. HONORÉ,
Thursday, Jan. 28th, 1847.

My dear Sir :

.   .   .   .   .   .

I was at Geneva at the time of the revolution.
The moderation and mildness of the successful party
were beyond all praise. Their appeals to the people of all parties—printed and pasted on the walls
—have no parallel that I know of, in history, for
their real good sterling Christianity and tendency
to promote the happiness of mankind. My sympathy is strongly with the Swiss radicals. They know
what Catholicity is ; they see, in some of their own
valleys, the poverty, ignorance, misery, and bigotry
it always brings in its train wherever it is triumphant ; and they would root it out of their children's way at any price. I fear the end of the struggle will be, that some Catholic power will step in to
crush the dangerously well-educated republics (very
dangerous to such neighbours) ; but there is a
spirit in the people, or I very much mistake them,

that will trouble the Jesuits there many years, and
shake their altar steps for them.

.   .   .   .   .   .

Ever believe me,
Cordially and truly yours.

[TO MR. W. C. MACREADY]

DEVONSHIRE TERRACE, Tuesday Morning, Nov. 23d, 1847.

My dear Macready :
I am in the whirlwind of finishing a number with
a crisis in it ; but I cannot fall to work without saying, in so many words, that I feel all words insuffi-
cient to tell you what I think of you after a night
like last night. The multitudes of new tokens by
which I know you for a great man, the swelling
within me of my love for you, the pride I have in
you, the majestic reflection I see in you of all the
passions and affections that make up our mystery,
throw me into a strange kind of transport that has
no expression but in a mute sense of an attachment,
which, in truth and fervency, is worthy of its subject.

What is this to say ? Nothing, God knows, and
yet I cannot leave it unsaid.

Ever affectionately yours.

P.S.—I never saw you more gallant and free than
in the gallant and free scenes last night. It was

perfectly captivating to behold you. However, it shall not interfere with my determination to address you as Old Parr in all future time.

[TO MR. W. C. MACREADY]

JUNCTION HOUSE, BRIGHTON, March 2d, 1848.

My dear Macready :

. . . . . .

I think Lamartine, so far, one of the best fellows in the world ; and I have lively hopes of that great people establishing a noble republic. Our court had best be careful not to overdo it in respect of sympathy with ex-royalty and ex-nobility. These are not times for such displays, as, it strikes me, the people in some of our great towns would be apt to express pretty plainly.

However, we'll talk of all this on these Sundays, and Mr. —— shall *not* be raised to the pinnacle of fame.

Ever affectionately yours,

My dear Macready.

[TO MR. ALEXANDER IRELAND]

DEVONSHIRE TERRACE, May 22d, 1848.

My dear Sir :

You very likely know that my company of amateurs have lately been playing, with a great reputation, in London here. The object is, "The endowment of a perpetual curatorship of Shakespeare's house, to be always held by some one distinguished in literature, and more especially in dramatic literature," and we have already a pledge from the Shakespeare House Committee that Sheridan Knowles shall be recommended to the Government as the first curator. This pledge, which is in the form of a minute, we intend to advertise in our country bills.

Now, on Monday, the 5th of June, we are going to play at Liverpool, where we are assured of a warm reception, and where an active committee for the issuing of tickets is already formed. Do you think the Manchester people would be equally glad to see us again, and that the house could be filled, as before, at our old prices? *If yes, would you and our other friends go, at once, to work in the cause?* The only night on which we could play in Manchester would be Saturday, the 3d of June. It is possible that the depression of the times may render a performance in Manchester unwise. In that case I would immediately abandon the idea.

. . . . . .

Faithfully yours always.

[TO MR. W. C. MACREADY]

BROADSTAIRS, KENT, Saturday, August 26th, 1848.

My dear Macready :

I was about to write to you when I received your welcome letter. You knew I should come from a somewhat longer distance than this to give you a hearty God-speed and farewell on the eve of your journey. What do you say to Monday, the fourth, or Saturday, the second ? Fix either day, let me know which suits you best—at what hour you expect the Inimitable, and the Inimitable will come up to the scratch like a man and a brother.

Permit me, in conclusion, to nail my colours to the mast. Stars and stripes are so-so—showy, perhaps ; but my colours is THE UNION JACK, which I am told has the remarkable property of having braved a thousand years the battle AND the breeze. Likewise, it is the flag of Albion—the standard of Britain ; and Britons, as I am informed, never, never, never—will—be—slaves !

My sentiment is : Success to the United States as a golden campaigning ground, but blow the United States to 'tarnal smash as an Englishman's place of residence. Gentlemen, are you all charged?

Affectionately ever.

[TO MISS DICKENS]

DEVONSHIRE TERRACE, Tuesday Night, Feb. 27th, 1849.

My dearest Mamey :
I am not engaged on the evening of your birthday. But even if I had an engagement of the most
particular kind, I should excuse myself from keeping
it, so that I might have the pleasure of celebrating
at home, and among my children, the day that gave
me such a dear and good daughter as you.

Ever affectionately yours.

[TO M. CERJAT]

DEVONSHIRE TERRACE, Saturday, Dec. 29th, 1849.

My dear Cerjat :
I received your letter at breakfast-time this morning with a pleasure my eloquence is unable to express and your modesty unable to conceive. It is
so delightful to be remembered at this time of the
year in your house where we have been so happy,
and in dear old Lausanne, that we always hope to
see again, that I can't help pushing away the first
page of *Copperfield* No. 10, now staring at me with
what I may literally call a blank aspect, and plung-
ing energetically into this reply.

What a strange coincidence that is about Blunderstone House! Of all the odd things I ever heard

(and their name is Legion), I think it is the oddest.
I went down into that part of the country on the
7th of January last year, when I was meditating the
story, and chose Blunderstone for the sound of its
name. I had previously observed much of what you
say about the poor girls. In all you suggest with
so much feeling about their return to virtue being
cruelly cut off, I concur with a sore heart. I have
been turning it over in my mind for some time, and
hope, in the history of little Em'ly (who *must* fall—
there is no hope for her), to put it before the
thoughts of people in a new and pathetic way, and
perhaps to do some good. You will be glad to hear,
I know, that *Copperfield* is a great success. I think
it is better liked than any of my other books.

We had a most delightful time at Watsons' (for
both of them we have preserved and strengthened a
real affection), and were the gayest of the gay.
There was a Miss Boyle staying in the house, who
is an excellent amateur actress, and she and I got
up some scenes from *The School for Scandal* and
from *Nickleby*, with immense success. We played
in the old hall, with the audience filled up and running over with servants. The entertainments concluded with feats of legerdemain (for the performance of which I have a pretty good apparatus, collected at divers times and in divers places), and we
then fell to country dances of a most frantic de-

scription, and danced all night. We often spoke of
you and Mrs. Cerjat and of Haldimand, and wished
you were all there. Watson and I have some fifty
times "registered a vow" (like O'Connell) to come
to Lausanne together, and have even settled in what
month and week. Something or other has always
interposed to prevent us; but I hope, please God,
most certainly to see it again, when my labours-
Copperfieldian shall have terminated.

You have no idea what the hanging of the Man-
nings really was. The conduct of the people was
so indescribably frightful, that I felt for some time
afterwards almost as if I were living in a city of
devils. I feel, at this hour, as if I never could go
near the place again. My letters have made a great
to-do and led to a great agitation of the subject;
but I have not a confident belief in any change
being made, mainly because the total abolitionists
are utterly reckless and dishonest (generally speaking), and would play the deuce with any such pro-
position in Parliament, unless it were strongly supported by the Government, which it would certainly
not be, the Whig motto (in office) being "*laissez
aller.*" I think Peel might do it if he came in.
Two points have occurred to me as being a good
commentary to the objections to my idea. The first
is that a most terrific uproar was made when the
hanging processions were abolished, and the cere-

mony shrunk from Tyburn to the prison door. The
second is that, at this very time, under the British
Government in New South Wales, executions take
place *within the prison walls*, with decidedly improved results. (I am waiting to explode this fact
on the first man of mark who gives me the opportunity.)

.   .   .   .   .   .

I do hope that we may all come together again
once more, while there is a head of hair left among
us ; and in this hope remain, my dear Cerjat,

Your faithful Friend.

[TO MR. CHARLES KNIGHT]

DEVONSHIRE TERRACE, February 8th, 1850.

My dear Knight :

Let me thank you in the heartiest manner for
your most kind and gratifying mention of me in
your able pamphlet. It gives me great pleasure, and
I sincerely feel it.

I quite agree with you in all you say so well of
the injustice and impolicy of this excessive taxation.
But when I think of the condition of the great mass
of the people, I fear that I could hardly feel the
heart to press for justice in this respect, before the
window-duty is removed. They cannot read without light. They cannot have an average chance of

life and health without it. Much as we feel our wrong, I fear that they feel their wrong more, and that the things just done in this wise must bear a new physical existence.

I never see you, and begin to think we must have another play—say in Cornwall—expressly to bring us together.

Very faithfully yours.

[TO MISS MARY BOYLE]

DEVONSHIRE TERRACE, Friday Night, late, Feb. 21st, 1851.

My dear Miss Boyle :

I have devoted a couple of hours this evening to going very carefully over your paper (which I had read before) and to endeavouring to bring it closer, and to lighten it, and to give it that sort of compactness which a habit of composition, and of disciplining one's thoughts like a regiment, and of studying the art of putting each soldier into his right place, may have gradually taught me to think necessary. I hope, when you see it in print, you will not be alarmed by my use of the pruning-knife. I have tried to exercise it with the utmost delicacy and discretion, and to suggest to you, especially towards the end, how this sort of writing (regard being had to the size of the journal in which it appears) requires to be compressed, and is made pleasanter by compression.

This all reads very solemnly, but only because I want you to read it (I mean the article) with as loving an eye as I have truly tried to touch it with a loving and gentle hand. I propose to call it "My Mahogany Friend." The other name is too long, and I think not attractive. Until I go to the office to-morrow and see what is actually in hand, I am not certain of the number in which it will appear, but Georgy shall write on Monday and tell you. We are always a fortnight in advance of the public, or the mechanical work could not be done. I think there are many things in it that are *very pretty.* The Katie part is particularly well done. If I don't say more, it is because I have a heavy sense, in all cases, of the responsibility of encouraging anyone to enter on that thorny track, where the prizes are so few and the blanks so many ; where——

But I won't write you a sermon. With the fire going out, and the first shadows of a new story hovering in a ghostly way about me (as they usually begin to do, when I have finished an old one), I am in danger of doing the heavy business, and becoming a heavy guardian, or something of that sort, instead of the light and airy Joe.

So good-night, and believe that you may always trust me, and never find a grim expression (towards you) in any that I wear.

Ever yours.

[TO THE HON. MRS. WATSON]

BROADSTAIRS, KENT, July 11th, 1851.

My dear Mrs. Watson :

.   .   .   .   .   .

To go to the opposite side of life, let me tell you
that a week or so ago I took Charley and three of
his schoolfellows down the river gipsying. I se-
cured the services of Charley's godfather (an old
friend of mine, and a noble fellow with boys), and
went down to Slough, accompanied by two immense
hampers from Fortnum and Mason, on (I believe) the
wettest morning ever seen out of the tropics. It
cleared before we got to Slough ; but the boys, who
had got up at four (we being due at eleven), had
horrible misgivings that we might not come, in consequence of which we saw them looking into the carriages before us, all face. They seemed to have no
bodies whatever, but to be all face ; their counte-
nances lengthened to that surprising extent. When
they saw us, the faces shut up as if they were upon
strong springs, and their waistcoats developed themselves in the usual places. When the first hamper
came out of the luggage-van, I was conscious of their
dancing behind the guard ; when the second came
out with bottles in it, they all stood wildly on one leg.
We then got a couple of flys to drive to the boat-

house. I put them in the first, but they couldn't
sit still a moment, and were perpetually flying up and
down like the toy figures in the sham snuff-boxes.
In this order we went on to "Tom Brown's, the
tailor's," where they all dressed in aquatic costume,
and then to the boat-house, where they all cried in
shrill chorus for "Mahogany"—a gentleman, so
called by reason of his sunburnt complexion, a water-
man by profession. (He was likewise called during
the day "Hog" and "Hogany," and seemed to be
unconscious of any proper name whatsoever.) We
embarked, the sun shining now, in a galley with a
striped awning, which I had ordered for the purpose,
and all rowing hard, went down the river. We
dined in a field ; what I suffered for fear those boys
should get drunk, the struggles I underwent in a
contest of feeling between hospitality and prudence,
must ever remain untold. I feel, even now, old with
the anxiety of that tremendous hour. They were
very good, however. The speech of one became
thick, and his eyes too like lobsters' to be comfortable, but only temporarily. He recovered, and I
suppose outlived the salad he took. I have heard
nothing to the contrary, and I imagine I should have
been implicated on the inquest if there had been
one. We had tea and rashers of bacon at a public-
house, and came home, the last five or six miles in
a prodigious thunderstorm. This was the great suc-

cess of the day, which they certainly enjoyed more
than anything else. The dinner had been great, and
Mahogany had informed them, after a bottle of light
champagne, that he never would come up the river
" with ginger company " any more. But the getting
so completely wet through was the culminating part
of the entertainment. You never in your life saw
such objects as they were, and their perfect uncon-
sciousness that it was at all advisable to go home
and change, or that there was anything to prevent
their standing at the station two mortal hours to
see me off, was wonderful. As to getting them to
their dames with any sort of sense that they were
damp, I abandoned the idea. I thought it a success
when they went down the street as civilly as if they
were just up and newly dressed, though they really
looked as if you could have rubbed them to rags
with a touch, like saturated curl-paper.

.   .   .   .

[TO MR. EELES]

" HOUSEHOLD WORDS " OFFICE,
Wednesday Evening, Oct. 22d, 1851.

Dear Mr. Eeles :

I send you the list I have made for the book-
backs. I should like the *History of a Short Chan-
cery Suit* to come at the bottom of one recess, and
the *Catalogue of Statues of the Duke of Wellington*
at the bottom of the other. If you should want

more titles, and will let me know how many, I will send them to you.

Faithfully yours.

LIST OF IMITATION BOOK-BACKS.

Tavistock House, 1851

Five Minutes in China. 3 vols.

Forty Winks at the Pyramids. 2 vols.

Abernethy on the Constitution. 2 vols.

Mr. Green's Overland Mail. 2 vols.

Captain Cook's Life of Savage. 2 vols.

A Carpenter's Bench of Bishops. 2 vols.

Toot's Universal Letter-Writer. 2 vols.

Orson's Art of Etiquette.

Downeaster's Complete Calculator.

History of the Middling Ages. 6 vols

Jonah's Account of the Whale.

Captain Parry's Virtues of Cold Tar.

Kant's Ancient Humbugs. 10 vols.

Bowwowdom. A Poem.

The Quarrelly Review. 4 vols.

The Gunpowder Magazine. 4 vols.

Steele. By the Author of *Ion*.

The Art of Cutting the Teeth.

Matthew's Nursery Songs. 2 vols.

Paxton's Bloomers. 5 vols.

On the Use of Mercury by the Ancient Poets.

Drowsy's Recollections of Nothing. 3 vols.

Heavyside's Conversations with Nobody. 3 vols.

Commonplace Book of the Oldest Inhabitant. 2 vols.

Growler's Gruffiology, with Appendix. 4 vols.

The Books of Moses and Sons. 2 vols.

Burke (of Edinburgh) on the Sublime and Beautiful. 2 vols.

Teazer's Commentaries.

King Henry the Eighth's Evidences of Christianity. 5 vols.

Miss Biffin on Deportment.

Morrison's Pills Progress. 2 vols.

Lady Godiva on the Horse.

Munchausen's Modern Miracles. 4 vols.

Richardson's Show of Dramatic Literature. 12 vols.

Hansard's Guide to Refreshing Sleep. As many volumes as possible.

[TO MRS. GASKELL]

TAVISTOCK HOUSE, Thursday Afternoon, Dec. 5th, 1851.

My dear Mrs. Gaskell :

I write in great haste to tell you that Mr. Wills, in the utmost consternation, has brought me your letter, just received (four o'clock), and that it is *too late* to recall your tale. I was so delighted with it that I put it first in the number (not hearing of any objection to my proposed alteration by return of post), and the number is now made up and in the printer's hands. I cannot possibly take the tale out —it has departed from me.

I am truly concerned for this, but I hope you will not blame me for what I have done in perfect good faith. Any recollection of me from your pen cannot (as I think you know) be otherwise than truly gratifying to me ; but with my name on every page of *Household Words,* there would be—or at least I should feel—an impropriety in so mentioning myself. I was particular, in changing the author, to make it " Hood's *Poems* " in the most important place—I mean where the captain is killed—and I hope and trust that the substitution will not be any serious drawback to the paper in any eyes but yours. I would do anything rather than cause you a minute's vexation arising out of what has given me so much pleasure, and I sincerely beseech you to think better of it, and not to fancy that any shade has been thrown on your charming writing, by

The unfortunate but innocent.

P.S.—I write at a gallop, not to loose another post.

TAVISTOCK HOUSE, Sunday, December 21st, 1851.

My dear Mrs. Gaskell :

If you were not the most suspicious of women, always looking for soft sawder in the purest metal of praise, I should call your paper delightful, and touched in the tenderest and most delicate manner. Being what you are, I confine myself to the observation that I have called it " A Love Affair at Cranford," and sent it off to the printer.

Faithfully yours ever.

TAVISTOCK HOUSE, TAVISTOCK SQUARE, July 9th, 1852.

Sir:

I have received your letter of yesterday's date, and shall content myself with a brief reply.

There was a long time during which benevolent

societies were spending immense sums on missions abroad, when there was no such thing as a ragged school in England, or any kind of associated endeavour to penetrate to those horrible domestic depths in which such schools are now to be found, and where they were, to my most certain knowledge, neither placed nor discovered by the Society for the Propagation of the Gospel in Foreign Parts.

If you think the balance between the home mission and the foreign mission justly held in the present time, I do not. I abstain from drawing the strange comparison that might be drawn between the sums even now expended in endeavours to remove the darkest ignorance and degradation from our very doors, because I have some respect for mistakes that may be founded in a sincere wish to do good. But I present a general suggestion of the still-existing anomaly (in such a paragraph as that which offends you), in the hope of inducing some people to reflect on this matter, and to adjust the balance more correctly. I am decidedly of opinion that the two works, the home and the foreign, are *not* conducted with an equal hand, and that the home claim is by far the stronger and the more pressing of the two.

Indeed, I have very grave doubts whether a great commercial country, holding communication with all parts of the world, can better Christianise the

benighted portions of it than by the bestowal of its
wealth and energy on the making of good Christians
at home, and on the utter removal of neglected and
untaught childhood from its streets, before it wan-
ders elsewhere. For, if it steadily persist in this
work, working downward to the lowest, the travellers of all grades whom it sends abroad will be
good, exemplary, practical missionaries, instead of
undoers of what the best professed missionaries
can do.

These are my opinions, founded, I believe, on
some knowledge of facts and some observation. If
I could be scared out of them, let me add in all
good humour, by such easily-impressed words as
"antichristian" or "irreligious," I should think that
I deserved them in their real signification.

I have referred in vain to page 312 of *Household
Words* for the sneer to which you call my attention. Nor have I, I assure you, the least idea where
else it is to be found.

I am, Sir, your faithful Servant.

[TO MR. W. H. WILLS]

HÔTEL DES BAINS, BOULOGNE, Tuesday, Oct. 12th, 1852.

My dear Wills :

H. W.

I have thought of the Christmas number, but not
very successfully, because I have been (and still am)

constantly occupied with *Bleak House.* I purpose
returning home either on Sunday or Monday, as
my work permits, and we will, immediately thereafter, dine at the office and talk it over, so that you
may get all the men to their work.

The fault of ——'s poem, besides its intrinsic
meanness as a composition, is that it goes too glibly
with the comfortable ideas (of which we have had a
great deal too much in England since the Continental commotions) that a man is to sit down and make
himself domestic and meek, no matter what is done
to him. It wants a stronger appeal to rulers in general to let men do this, fairly, by governing them
well. As it stands, it is at about the tract-mark
(*Dairyman's Daughter*, etc.) of political morality,
and don't think that it is necessary to write *down* to
any part of our audience. I always hold that to be
as great a mistake as can be made.

I wish you would mention to Thomas, that I think
the paper on hops *extremely well done.* He has
quite caught the idea we want, and caught it in the
best way. In pursuing the bridge subject, I think
it would be advisable to look up the *Thames police.*
I have a misty notion of some capital papers coming
out of it. Will you see to this branch of the tree
among the other branches?

6

MYSELF.

To Chapman I will write. My impression is that
I shall not subscribe to the Hood monument, as I
am not at all favourable to such posthumous hon-
ours.

Ever faithfully. .

[TO MR. W. H. WILLS]

HÔTEL DES BAINS, BOULOGNE,
Wednesday Night, Oct. 13th, 1852.

My dear Wills :

The number coming in after dinner, since my
letter was written and posted, I have gone over it.

I am grievously depressed by it ; it is so exceedingly bad. If you have anything else to put first,
don't put ——'s paper first. (There is nothing better for a beginning in the number as it stands, but
this is very bad.) It is a mistake to think of it as a
first article. The article itself is in the main a mistake. Firstly, the subject requires the greatest discretion and nicety of touch. And secondly, it is
all wrong and self-contradictory. Nobody can for a
moment suppose that "sporting" amusements are
the sports of the PEOPLE ; the whole gist of the best
part of the description is to show that they are the
amusements of a peculiar and limited class. The
greater part of them are at a miserable discount

(horse-racing excepted, which has already been sufficiently done in H. W.), and there is no reason for running amuck at them at all. I have endeavoured to remove much of my objection (and I think have done so), but, both in purpose and in any general address, it is as wide of a first article as anything can well be. It would do best in the opening of the number.

About Sunday in Paris there is no kind of doubt. Take it out. Such a thing as that crucifixion, unless it were done in a masterly manner, we have no business to stagger families with. Besides, the name is a comprehensive one, and should include a quantity of fine matter. Lord bless me, what I could write under that head !

Strengthen the number, pray, by anything good you may have. It is a very dreary business as it stands.

The proofs want a thorough revision.

In haste, going to bed.

Ever faithfully.

P.S.—I want a name for Miss Martineau's paper.

TRIUMPHANT CARRIAGES (or TRIUMPHAL).
DUBLIN STOUTHEARTEDNESS.
PATIENCE AND PREJUDICE.

Take which you like best.

[TO MR. JOHN WATKINS]

MONDAY, October 18th, 1852.

Sir :

On my return to town I find the letter awaiting me which you did me the favour to address to me, I believe—for it has no date—some days ago.

I have the greatest tenderness for the memory of Hood, as I had for himself. But I am not very favourable to posthumous memorials in the monument way, and I should exceedingly regret to see any such appeal as you contemplate made public, remembering another public appeal that was made and responded to after Hood's death. I think that I best discharge my duty to my deceased friend, and best consult the respect and love with which I remember him, by declining to join in any such public endeavours as that which you (in all generosity and singleness of purpose, I am sure) advance. I shall have a melancholy gratification in privately assisting to place a simple and plain record over the remains of a great writer that should be as modest as he was himself, but I regard any other monument in connection with his mortal resting-place as a mistake.

I am, Sir, your faithful servant.

ATHENÆUM, Monday, November 22d, 1852.

My dear Mrs. Watson:
Having just now finished my work for the time
being, I turn in here in the course of a rainy walk,
to have the gratification of writing a few lines to
you. If my occupations with this same right hand
were less numerous, you would soon be tired of me,
I should write to you so often. You asked Catherine a question about *Bleak House*. Its circulation is half as large again as *Copperfield!* I have
just now come to the point I have been patiently
working up to in the writing, and I hope it will
suggest to you a pretty and affecting thing. In
the matter of *Uncle Tom's Cabin*, I partly though
not entirely agree with Mr. James. No doubt a
much lower art will serve for the handling of such a
subject in fiction, than for a launch on the sea of
imagination without such a powerful bark; but
there are many points in the book very admirably
done. There is a certain St. Clair, a New Orleans
gentleman, who seems to me to be conceived with
great power and originality. If he had not "a
Grecian outline of face," which I began to be a little
tired of in my earliest infancy, I should think him
unexceptionable. He has a sister too, a maiden

lady from New England, in whose person the beset-
ting weaknesses and prejudices of the Abolitionists
themselves, on the subject of the blacks, are set
forth in the liveliest and truest colours and with the
greatest boldness.

.   .   .   .   .   .

I am ever, with the best and truest wishes of my
heart, my dear Mrs. Watson,

Your most affectionate Friend.

[TO MR. W. WILKIE COLLINS]

TAVISTOCK HOUSE, Monday, Dec. 20th, 1852.

My dear Collins :

If I did not know that you are likely to have
a forbearing remembrance of my occupation, I
should be full of remorse for not having sooner
thanked you for *Basil.*

Not to play the sage or the critic (neither of
which parts, I hope, is at all in my line), but to say
what is the friendly truth, I may assure you that I
have read the book with very great interest, and
with a very thorough conviction that you have a
call to this same art of fiction. I think the proba-
bilities here and there require a little more respect
than you are disposed to show them, and I have no
doubt that the prefatory letter would have been
better away, on the ground that a book (of all

things) should speak for and explain itself. But the story contains admirable writing, and many clear evidences of a very delicate discrimination of character. It is delightful to find throughout that you have taken great pains with it besides, and have "gone at it" with a perfect knowledge of the jolter-headedness of the conceited idots who suppose that volumes are to be tossed off like pancakes, and that any writing can be done without the utmost application, the greatest patience, and the steadiest energy of which the writer is capable.

For all these reasons, I have made *Basil's* acquaintance with great gratification, and entertain a high respect for him. And I hope that I shall become intimate with many worthy descendants of his, who are yet in the limbo of creatures waiting to be born.

Always faithfully yours.

[TO MR. CLARKSON STANFIELD]

H.M.S. Tavistock, January 3d, 1853.

Yoho, old salt! Neptun' ahoy! You don't forget, messmet, as you was to meet Dick Sparkler and Mark Porpuss on the fok'sle of the good ship *Owssel Words*, Wednesday next, half-past four? Not you; for when did Stanfell ever pass his word to go anywheers and not come! Well. Belay, my heart of oak, belay! Come alongside the *Tavistock* same day and hour, 'stead of *Owssel Words.* Hail your shipmets, and they'll drop over the side and join you, like two new shillings a-droppin' into the purser's pocket. Damn all lubberly boys and swabs, and give *me* the lad with the tarry trousers, which shines to me like di'mings bright!

[TO MR. WALTER SAVAGE LANDOR]

TAVISTOCK HOUSE, LONDON, Sept. 8th, 1853.

My dear Landor :

I am in town for a day or two, and Forster tells me I may now write to thank you for the happiness you have given me by honouring my name with such generous mention, on such a noble place, in your great book. I believe he has told you already that I wrote to him from Boulogne, not knowing what to do, as I had not received the precious volume, and feared you might have some plan of sending it to me, with which my premature writing would interfere.

You know how heartily and inexpressibly I prize what you have written to me, or you never would have selected me for such a distinction. I could never thank you enough, my dear Landor, and I will not thank you in words any more. Believe me, I receive the dedication like a great dignity, the worth of which I hope I thoroughly know. The Queen could give me none in exchange that I wouldn't laughingly snap my fingers at.

. . . . .

Ever, my dear Landor,
Heartily and affectionately yours.

[TO MISS HOGARTH]

HÔTEL DES ÉTRANGERS, NAPLES,
Friday Night, Nov. 4th, 1853.

My dearest Georgy :

Instead of embarking on Monday at Genoa, we were delayed (in consequence of the boat's being a day later when there are thirty-one days in the month) until Tuesday. Going aboard that morning at half-past nine, we found the steamer more than full of passengers from Marseilles, and in a state of confusion not to be described. We could get no places at the table, got our dinners how we could on deck, had no berths or sleeping accommodation of any kind, and had paid heavy first-class fares! To add to this, we got to Leghorn too late to steam away again that night, getting the ship's papers examined first—as the authorities said so, not being favourable to the new express English ship, English officered—and we lay off the lighthouse all night long. The scene on board beggars description. Ladies on the tables, gentlemen under the tables,

and ladies and gentlemen lying indiscriminately on
the open deck, arrayed like spoons on a sideboard.
No mattresses, no blankets, nothing. Towards midnight, attempts were made by means of an awning and flags to make this latter scene remotely approach an Australian encampment ; and we three
lay together on the bare planks covered with over-
coats. We were all gradually dozing off when a perfectly tropical rain fell, and in a moment drowned
the whole ship. The rest of the night was passed
upon the stairs, with an immense jumble of men
and women. When anybody came up for any
purpose we all fell down ; and when anybody came
down we all fell up again. Still, the good-humour
in the English part of the passengers was quite extraordinary. There were excellent officers aboard,
and the first mate lent me his cabin to wash in in
the morning, which I afterwards lent to Egg and
Collins. Then we and the Emerson Tennents (who
were aboard) and the captain, the doctor, and the
second officer went off on a jaunt together to Pisa,
as the ship was to lie at Leghorn all day.

The captain was a capital fellow, but I led him,
facetiously, such a life all day, that I got almost
everything altered at night. Emerson Tennent,
with the greatest kindness, turned his son out of
his state-room (who, indeed, volunteered to go in
the most amiable manner), and I got a good bed

there. The store-room down by the hold was opened for Egg and Collins, and they slept with tho moist sugar, the cheese in cut, the spices, the cruets, the apples and pears—in a perfect chandler's shop; in company with what the ——'s would call a "hold gent"—who had been so horribly wet through overnight that his condition frightened the authorities—a cat, and the steward—who dozed in an arm-chair, and all night long fell headforemost, once in every five minutes, on Egg, who slept on the counter or dresser. Last night I had the steward's own cabin, opening on deck, all to myself. It had been previously occupied by some desolate lady, who went ashore at Civita Vecchia. There was little or no sea, thank Heaven, all the trip; but the rain was heavier than any I have ever seen, and the lightning very constant and vivid. We were, with the crew, some two hundred people; with boats, at the utmost stretch, for one hundred, perhaps. I could not help thinking what would happen if we met with any accident; the crew being chiefly Maltese, and evidently fellows who would cut off alone in the largest boat on the least alarm. The speed (it being the crack express ship for the India mail) very high; also the running through all the narrow rocky channels. Thank God, however, here we are. Though the more sensible and experienced part of the passengers agreed with me this morning that it was not a thing to try often. We had an excellent table after the first day, the best wines and so forth, and the captain and I swore eternal friendship. Ditto the first officer and the majority of the passengers. We got into the bay about seven this morning, but could not land until noon. We towed from Civita Vecchia the entire Greek navy, I believe, consisting of a little brig-of-war, with great guns, fitted as a steamer, but disabled by having burst the bottom of her boiler in her first run. She was just big enough to carry the captain and a crew of six or so, but the captain was so covered with buttons and gold that there never would have been room for him on board to put these valuables away if he hadn't worn them, which he consequently did, all night.

.   .   .   .   .   .

I am afraid this is a dull letter, for I am very tired. You must take the will for the deed, my dear, and good night.

Ever most affectionately.

.

[TO MR. W. H. WILLS]

ROME, Thursday Afternoon, Nov. 17th, 1853.

My dear Wills :

.   .   .   .   .   .

KEEP *Household Words* IMAGINATIVE ! is the solemn and continual Conductorial Injunction. Delighted to hear of Mrs. Gaskell's contributions.

.

Yes by all manners of means to Lady Holland. Will you ask her whether she has Sydney Smith's letters to me, which I placed (at Mrs. Smith's request) either in Mrs. Smith's own hands or in Mrs. Austin's? I cannot remember which, but I think the latter.

In making up the Christmas number, don't consider my paper or papers, with any reference saving to where they will fall best. I have no liking, in the case, for any particular place.

All perfectly well. Companion moustaches (particularly Egg's) dismal in the extreme. Kindest regards to Mrs. Wills.

Ever faithfully.

[TO MR. CHARLES KNIGHT]

TAVISTOCK HOUSE, January 30th, 1854.

My dear Knight :

Indeed there is no fear of my thinking you the owner of a cold heart. I am more than three parts disposed, however, to be ferocious with you for ever writing down such a preposterous truism.

My satire is against those who see figures and averages, and nothing else—the representatives of the wickedest and most enormous vice of this time —the men who, through long years to come, will do more to damage the real useful truths of politi-

cal economy than I could do (if I tried) in my whole
life; the addled heads who would take the average
of cold in the Crimea during twelve months as a
reason for clothing a soldier in nankeens on a night
when he would be frozen to death in fur, and who
would comfort the labourer in travelling twelve
miles a day to and from his work, by telling him
that the average distance of one inhabited place
from another in the whole area of England, is not
more than four miles. Bah! What have you to do
with these?

I shall put the book upon a private shelf (after
reading it) by *Once upon a Time.* I should have
buried my pipe of peace and sent you this blast of
my war-horn three or four days ago, but that I have
been reading to a little audience of three thousand
five hundred at Bradford.

Ever affectionately yours.

[TO MISS HOGARTH]

OFFICE OF "HOUSEHOLD WORDS," Saturday, July 22d, 1854.

My dear Georgina :
Neither you nor Catherine did justice to Collins's
book.[1] I think it far away the cleverest novel I
have ever seen written by a new hand. It is in
some respects masterly. Valentine Blyth is as orig-

---

[1] *Hide and Seek.*

inal, and as well done as anything can be. The scene where he shows his pictures is full of an admirable humour. Old Mat is admirably done. In short, I call it a very remarkable book, and have been very much surprised by its great merit.

Tell Kate, with my love, that she will receive to-morrow in a little parcel, the complete proofs of *Hard Times.* They will not be corrected, but she will find them pretty plain. I am just now going to put them up for her. I saw Grisi the night before last in *Lucrezia Borgia*—finer than ever. Last night I was drinking gin-slings till daylight, with Buckstone of all people, who saw me looking at the Spanish dancers, and insisted on being convivial. I have been in a blaze of dissipation altogether, and have succeeded (I think), in knocking the remembrance of my work out.

Loves to all the darlings, from the Plornish-Maroon upward. London is far hotter than Naples.

Ever affectionately.

[TO THE HON. MRS. WATSON]

TAVISTOCK HOUSE, Wednesday, Nov. 1st, 1854.

My dear Mrs. Watson:

I take upon myself to answer your letter to Catherine, as I am referred to in it.

The Walk is not my writing. It is very well

done by a close imitator. Why I found myself so
"used up" after *Hard Times* I scarcely know,
perhaps because I intended to do nothing in that
way for a year, when the idea laid hold of me by
the throat in a very violent manner, and because
the compression and close condensation necessary
for that disjointed form of publication gave me perpetual trouble. But I really was tired, which is a
result so very incomprehensible that I can't forget
it. I have passed an idle autumn in a beautiful
situation, and am dreadfully brown and big. For
further particulars of Boulogne, see "Our French
Watering Place," in this present week of *Household
Words* which contains a faithful portrait of our
landlord there.

.   .   .   .   .   .

I am full of mixed feeling about the war—admiration of our valiant men, burning desires to cut the
Emperor of Russia's throat, and something like de-
spair to see how the old cannon-smoke and blood-
mists obscure the wrongs and sufferings of the people at home. When I consider the Patriotic Fund
on the one hand, and on the other the poverty and
wretchedness engendered by cholera, of which in
London alone, an infinitely larger number of English people than are likely to be slain in the whole
Russian war have miserably and needlessly died—
I feel as if the world had been pushed back five

hundred years. If you are reading new books just now, I think you will be interested with a controversy between Whewell and Brewster, on the question of the shining orbs about us being inhabited or no. Whewell's book is called, *On the Plurality of Worlds ;* Brewster's, *More Worlds than One.* I shouldn't wonder if you know all about them. They bring together a vast number of points of great interest in natural philosophy, and some very curious reasoning on both sides, and leave the matter pretty much where it was.

.   .   .   .   .   .

Dr. Rae's account of Franklin's unfortunate party is deeply interesting ; but I think hasty in its acceptance of details, particularly in the statement that they had eaten the dead bodies of their companions, which I don't believe. Franklin, on a former occasion, was almost starved to death, had gone through all the pains of that sad end, and lain down to die, and no such thought had presented itself to any of them. In famous cases of shipwreck, it is very rare indeed that any person of any humanising education or refinement resorts to this dreadful means of prolonging life. In open boats, the coarsest and commonest men of the shipwrecked party have done such things ; but I don't remember more than one instance in which an officer had overcome the loathing that the idea had inspired. Dr.

7

Rae talks about their *cooking* these remains too. I should like to know where the fuel came from.

Kindest love and best regards.

Ever, my dear Mrs. Watson, affectionately yours.

[TO M. DE CERJAT]

TAVISTOCK HOUSE, January 3d, 1855.

My dear Cerjat :

When your Christmas letter did not arrive according to custom, I felt as if a bit of Christmas had fallen out and there was no supplying the piece.   However, it was soon supplied by yourself, and the bowl became round and sound again.

.   .   .   .   .   .

The absorption of the English mind in the war is, to me, a melancholy thing.   Every other subject of popular solicitude and sympathy goes down before it.   I fear I clearly see that for years to come domestic reforms are shaken to the root ; every miserable red-tapist flourishes war over the head of every protester against his humbug ; and everything connected with it is pushed to such an unreasonable extent, that, however kind and necessary it may be in itself, it becomes ridiculous.   For all this it is an indubitable fact, I conceive, that Russia MUST BE stopped, and that the future peace of the world renders the war imperative upon us.   The

Duke of Newcastle lately addressed a private letter
to the newspapers, entreating them to exercise a
larger discretion in respect of the letters of "Our
Own Correspondents," against which Lord Raglan
protests as giving the Emperor of Russia information for nothing which would cost him (if indeed
he could get it at all) fifty or a hundred thousand
pounds a year. The communication has not been
attended with much effect, so far as I can see. In
the meantime I do suppose we have the wretchedest
Ministry that ever was—in whom nobody not in
office of some sort believes—yet whom there is
nobody to displace. The strangest result, perhaps,
of years of Reformed Parliaments that ever the
general sagacity did *not* foresee.

Let me recommend you, as a brother-reader of
high distinction, two comedies, both Goldsmith's—
She Stoops to Conquer and *The Good-natured Man*.
Both are so admirable and so delightfully written
that they read wonderfully. A friend of mine, Forster, who wrote *The Life of Goldsmith*, was very ill
a year or so ago, and begged me to read to him one
night as he lay in bed, "something of Goldsmith's."
I fell upon *She Stoops to Conquer*, and we enjoyed it
with that wonderful intensity, that I believe he began to get better in the first scene, and was all right
again in the fifth act.

I am charmed by your account of Haldimand, to

whom my love. Tell him Sydney Smith's daughter has privately printed a life of her father with selections from his letters, which has great merit, and often presents him exactly as he used to be. I have strongly urged her to publish it, and I think she will do so, about March.

My eldest boy has come home from Germany to learn a business life at Birmingham (I think), first of all. The whole nine are well and happy. Ditto, Mrs. Dickens. Ditto, Georgina. My two girls are full of interest in yours ; and one of mine (as I think I told you when I was at Élysée) is curiously like one of yours in the face. They are all agog now about a great fairy play, which is to come off here next Monday. The house is full of spangles, gas, Jew theatrical tailors, and pantomime carpenters. We all unite in kindest and best loves to dear Mrs. Cerjat, and all the blooming daughters. And I am, with frequent thoughts of you and cordial affection, ever, my dear Cerjat,

Your faithful Friend.

[TO MR. ARTHUR RYLAND]

TAVISTOCK HOUSE, Monday, Jan. 29th, 1855.

My dear Mr. Ryland :

I have been in the greatest difficulty—which I am not yet out of—to know what to read at Bir-

mingham. I fear the idea of next month is now
impracticable. Which of two other months do you
think would be preferable for your Birmingham
objects? Next May, or next December?

Having already read two Christmas books at Birmingham, I should like to get out of that restric-
tion, and have a swim in the broader waters of one
of my long books. I have been poring over *Copperfield* (which is my favourite), with the idea of getting a reading out of it, to be called by some such
name as *Young Housekeeping and Little Emily*.
But there is still the huge difficulty that I con-
structed the whole with immense pains, and have
so woven it up and blended it together, that I cannot yet so separate the parts as to tell the story of
David's married life with Dora, and the story of Mr.
Peggotty's search for his niece, within the time.
This is my object. If I could possibly bring it to
bear, it would make a very attractive reading, with
a strong interest in it, and a certain completeness.

This is exactly the state of the case. I don't
mind confiding to you, that I never can approach
the book with perfect composure (it had such perfect possession of me when I wrote it), and that I
no sooner begin to try to get it into this form,
than I begin to read it all, and to feel that I cannot
disturb it. I have not been unmindful of the
agreement we made at parting, and I have sat star-

ing at the backs of my books for an inspiration. This project is the only one that I have constantly reverted to, and yet I have made no progress in it!

Faithfully yours always.

[TO MR. DAVID ROBERTS, R.A.]

TAVISTOCK HOUSE, February 28th, 1855.

My dear David Roberts :

I hope to make it quite plain to you, in a few words, why I think it right to stay away from the Lord Mayor's dinner to the club. If I did not feel a kind of rectitude involved in my non-acceptance of his invitation, your note would immediately induce me to change my mind.

Entertaining a strong opinion on the subject of the City Corporation as it stands, and the absurdity of its pretensions in an age perfectly different, in all conceivable respects, from that to which it properly belonged as a reality, I have expressed that opinion on more than one occasion, within a year or so, in *Household Words.* I do not think it consistent with my respect for myself, or for the art I profess, to blow hot and cold in the same breath ; and to laugh at the institution in print, and accept the hospitality of its representative while the ink is staring us all in the face. There is a great deal too much of this among us, and it does not elevate the earnestness or delicacy of literature.

This is my sole consideration. Personally I have always met the present Lord Mayor on the most agreeable terms, and I think him an excellent one. As between you, and me, and him, I cannot have the slightest objection to your telling him the truth. On a more private occasion, when he was not keeping his state, I should be delighted to interchange any courtesy with that honourable and amiable gentleman, Mr. Moon.

Believe me always cordially yours.

[TO MR. W. M. THACKERAY]

TAVISTOCK HOUSE, Friday Evening, 23d March, 1855.

My dear Thackeray :

I have read in *The Times* to-day an account of your last night's lecture, and cannot refrain from assuring you in all truth and earnestness that I am profoundly touched by your generous reference to me. I do not know how to tell you what a glow it spread over my heart. Out of its fulness I do entreat you to believe that I shall never forget your words of commendation. If you could wholly know at once how you have moved me, and how you have animated me, you would be the happier I am very certain.

Faithfully yours ever.

Tuesday, 3d April, 1855.

My dear Maria:

A necessity is upon me now—as at most times—of wandering about in my old wild way, to think. I could no more resist this on Sunday or yesterday than a man can dispense with food, or a horse can help himself from being driven. I hold my inventive capacity on the stern condition that it must master my whole life, often have complete possession of me, make its own demands upon me, and sometimes, for months together, put everything else away from me. If I had not known long ago that my place could never be held, unless I were at any moment ready to devote myself to it entirely, I should have dropped out of it very soon. All this I can hardly expect you to understand—or the restlessness and waywardness of an author's mind. You have never seen it before you, or lived with it, or had occasion to think or care about it, and you cannot have the necessary consideration for it. "It is only half-an-hour,"—"It is only an afternoon,"—"It is only an evening," people say to me over and over again ; but they don't know that it is impossible to command one's self sometimes to any stipu-

[1] Mrs. Winter, a very dear friend and companion of Charles Dickens in his youth.

lated and set disposal of five minutes,—or that the mere consciousness of an engagement will sometimes worry a whole day. These are the penalties paid for writing books. Whoever is devoted to an art must be content to deliver himself wholly up to it, and to find his recompense in it. I am grieved if you suspect me of not wanting to see you, but I can't help it ; I must go my way whether or no.

.   .   .   .   .   .

Ever affectionately.

[TO MR. AUSTEN H. LAYARD]

TAVISTOCK HOUSE, Tuesday, April 10th, 1855.

Dear Layard :

I shall of course observe the strictest silence at present, in reference to your resolutions. It will be a most acceptable occupation to me to go over them with you, and I have not a doubt of their producing a strong effect out of doors.

There is nothing in the present time at once so galling and so alarming to me as the alienation of the people from their own public affairs. I have no difficulty in understanding it. They have had so little to do with the game through all these years of Parliamentary Reform, that they have sullenly laid down their cards, and taken to looking on. The players who are left at the table do not see beyond it, conceive that gain and loss and all the interest of the play are in their hands, and will never be wiser until they and the table and the lights and the money are all overturned together. And I believe the discontent to be so much the worse for smouldering, instead of blazing openly, that it is extremely like the general mind of France before the breaking out of the first Revolution, and is in danger of being turned by any one of a thousand accidents—a bad harvest—the last strain too much of aristocratic insolence or incapacity—a defeat abroad—a mere chance at home—with such a devil of a conflagration as never has been beheld since.

Meanwhile, all our English tuft-hunting, toad-eating, and other manifestations of accursed gentility—to say nothing of the Lord knows who's defiances of the proven truth before six hundred and fifty men—ARE expressing themselves every day. So, every day, the disgusted millions with this unnatural gloom are confirmed and hardened in the very worst of moods. Finally, round all this is an atmosphere of poverty, hunger, and ignorant desperation, of the mere existence of which perhaps not one man in a thousand of those not actually enveloped in it, through the whole extent of this country, has the least idea.

It seems to me an absolute impossibility to direct the spirit of the people at this pass until it shows it-

self. If they begin to bestir themselves in the vigorous national manner ; if they would appear in political reunion, array themselves peacefully but in
vast numbers against a system that they know to be
rotten altogether, make themselves heard like the
sea all round this island, I for one should be in
such a movement heart and soul, and should think
it a duty of the plainest kind to go along with it,
and try to guide it by all possible means. But you
can no more help a people who do not help themselves than you can help a man who does not help
himself. And until the people can be got up from
the lethargy, which is an awful symptom of the advanced state of their disease, I know of nothing that
can be done beyond keeping their wrongs continu-
ally before them.

I shall hope to see you soon after you come back.
Your speeches at Aberdeen are most admirable,
manful, and earnest. I would have such speeches
at every market-cross, and in every town-hall, and
among all sorts and conditions of men ; up in the
very balloons, and down in the very diving-bells.

Ever, cordially yours.

[TO MRS. TROLLOPE]

TAVISTOCK HOUSE, Tuesday Morning, June 19th, 1855.

My dear Mrs. Trollope :

I was out of town on Sunday, or I should have answered your note immediately on its arrival. I cannot have the pleasure of seeing the famous " medium " to-night, for I have some theatricals at home. But I fear I shall not in any case be a good subject for the purpose, as I altogether want faith in the thing.

I have not the least belief in the awful unseen world being available for evening parties at so much per night ; and, although I should be ready to receive enlightenment from any source, I must say I have very little hope of it from the spirits who express themselves through mediums, as I have never yet observed them to talk anything but nonsense, of which (as Carlyle would say) there is probably enough in these days of ours, and in all days, among mere mortality.

Very faithfully yours.

[TO MR. W. C. MACREADY]

FOLKESTONE, Thursday, Oct. 4th, 1855.

My dearest Macready :

I have been hammering away in that strenuous manner at my book, that I have had leisure for scarcely any letters but such as I have been obliged to write ; having a horrible temptation when I lay down my book-pen to run out on the breezy down here, tear up the hills, slide down the same, and conduct myself in a frenzied manner, for the relief that only exercise gives me.

.   .   .   .   .   .

As to the suffrage, I have lost hope even in the ballot. We appear to me to have proved the failure of representative institutions without an educated and advanced people to support them. What with teaching people to "keep in their stations," what with bringing up the soul and body of the land to be a good child, or to go to the beershop, to go a-poaching and go to the devil ; what with having no such thing as a middle class (for though we are perpetually bragging of it as our safety, it is nothing but a poor fringe on the mantle of the upper) ; what with flunkyism, toadyism, letting the most contemptible lords come in for all manner of places, reading *The Court Circular* for the New Testament, I do reluctantly believe that the English people are habitually consenting parties to the miserable imbecility into which we have fallen, *and never will help themselves out of it*. Who is to do it, if anybody is, God knows. But at present we are on the down-hill road to being conquered, and the people

WILL be content to bear it, sing "Rule Britannia,"
and WILL NOT be saved.

In No. 3 of my new book I have been blowing
off a little of indignant steam which would otherwise blow me up, and with God's leave I shall
walk in the same all the days of my life; but
I have no present political faith or hope—not a
grain.

I am going to read the *Carol* here to-morrow
in a long carpenter's shop, which looks far more
alarming as a place to hear in than the Town Hall
at Birmingham.

Kindest loves from all to your dear sister, Kate
and the darlings. It is blowing a gale here from
the south-west and raining like mad.

Ever most affectionately.

[TO MR. W. H. WILLS]   .

40, AVENUE DES CHAMPS ÉLYSÉES,
Wednesday, Oct. 24th, 1855.

My dear Wills :

In the Gad's Hill matter, I too would like to try
the effect of "not budging." *So do not go beyond
the* £1,700. Considering what I should have to expend on the one hand, and the low price of stock
on the other, I do not feel disposed to go beyond
that mark. They won't let a purchaser escape for

the sake of the £100, I think. And Austin was strongly of opinion, when I saw him last, that £1,700 was enough.

You cannot think how pleasant it is to me to find myself generally known and liked here. If I go into a shop to buy anything, and give my card, the officiating priest or priestess brightens up, and says : " *Ah! c'est l'écrivain célèbre! Monsieur porte un nom très-distingué. Mais ! je suis honoré et intéressé de voir Monsieur Dick-in. Je lis un des livres de monsieur tous les jours* " (in the *Moniteur*). And a man who brought some little vases home last night, said : " *On connaît bien en France que Monsieur Dick-in prend sa position sur la dignité de la littérature. Ah ! c'est grande chose ! Et ses caractères* " (this was to Georgina, while he unpacked) " *sont si spirituellement tournés ! Cette Madame Tojare* " (Todgers) " *ah ! qu'elle est drôle et précisément comme une dame que je connais à Calais.*"

You cannot have any doubt about this place, if you will only recollect it is the great main road from the Place de la Concorde to the Barrière de l'Étoile.

Ever faithfully.

[TO MONSIEUR REGNIER]

Wednesday, November 21st, 1855.

My dear Regnier:

In thanking you for the box you kindly sent me the day before yesterday, let me thank you a thousand times for the delight we derived from the representation of your beautiful and admirable piece. I have hardly ever been so affected, and interested in any theatre. Its construction is in the highest degree excellent, the interest absorbing, and the whole conducted by a masterly hand to a touching and natural conclusion.

Through the whole story from beginning to end, I recognise the true spirit and feeling of an artist, and I most heartily offer you and your fellow-labourer my felicitations on the success you have achieved. That it will prove a very great and a lasting one, I cannot for a moment doubt.

Oh my friend! If I could see an English actress with but one hundredth part of the nature and art of Madame Plessy, I should believe our English theatre to be in a fair way towards its regeneration. But I have no hope of ever beholding such a phenomenon. I may as well expect ever to see upon an English stage an accomplished artist, able to write and to embody what he writes, like you.

Faithfully yours ever.

[TO MADAME VIARDOT]

49, Avenue des Champs Élysées, Monday, Dec. 3d, 1855.

Dear Madame Viardot :

Mrs. Dickens tells me that you have only bor-
rowed the first number of *Little Dorrit*, and are
going to send it back. Pray do nothing of the
sort, and allow me to have the great pleasure of
sending you the succeeding numbers as they reach
me. I have had such delight in your great genius,
and have so high an interest in it and admiration of
it, that I am proud of the honour of giving you a
moment's intellectual pleasure.

Believe me, very faithfully yours.

[TO MR. MARK LEMON]

49, Champs Élysées, Paris, Monday, Jan. 7th, 1856.

My dear Mark :

I want to know how *Jack and the Beanstalk* goes.
I have a notion from a notice—a favourable notice,
however—which I saw in *Galignani*, that Webster
has let down the comic business.

In a piece at the Ambigu, called the *Rentrée à
Paris*, a mere scene in honour of the return of the
troops from the Crimea the other day, there is a
novelty which I think it worth letting you know of,

8

as it is easily available, either for a serious or a comic interest—the introduction of a supposed electric telegraph. The scene is the railway terminus at Paris, with the electric telegraph office on the prompt side, and the clerks *with their backs to the audience*—much more real than if they were, as they infallibly would be, staring about the house—working the needles ; and the little bell perpetually ringing. There are assembled to greet the soldiers, all the easily and naturally imagined elements of interest—old veteran fathers, young children, agonised mothers, sisters and brothers, girl lovers— each impatient to know of his or her own object of solicitude. Enter to these a certain marquis, full of sympathy for all, who says : " My friends, I am one of you. My brother has no commission yet. He is a common soldier. I wait for him as well as all brothers and sisters here wait for *their* brothers. Tell me whom you are expecting." Then they all tell him. Then he goes into the telegraph-office, and sends a message down the line to know how long the troops will be. Bell rings. Answer handed out on a slip of paper. "Delay on the line. Troops will not arrive for a quarter of an hour." General disappointment. "But we have this brave electric telegraph, my friends," says the marquis. "Give me your little messages, and I'll send them off." General rush round the marquis. Exclama-

tions : "How's Henri?" "My love to Georges;"
"Has Guillaume forgotten Élise?" "Is my son
wounded?" "Is my brother promoted?" etc. etc.
Marquis composes tumult. Sends message—such
a regiment, such a company, "Élise's love to
Georges." Little bell rings, slip of paper handed
out—"Georges in ten minutes will embrace his
Élise. Sends her a thousand kisses." Marquis
sends message—such a regiment, such a company—
"Is my son wounded?" Little bell rings. Slip of
paper handed out—"No. He has not yet upon
him those marks of bravery in the glorious service
of his country which his dear old father bears"
(father being lamed and invalided). Last of all, the
widowed mother. Marquis sends message—such
a regiment, such a company—"Is my only son
safe?" Little bell rings. Slip of paper handed
out—"He was first upon the heights of Alma."
General cheer. Bell rings again, another slip of
paper handed out. "He was made a sergeant at
Inkermann." Another cheer. Bell rings again, another slip of paper handed out. "He was made
colour - sergeant at Sebastopol." Another cheer.
Bell rings again, another slip of paper handed out.
"He was the first man who leaped with the French
banner on the Malakhoff tower." Tremendous
cheer. Bell rings again, another slip of paper
handed out. "But he was struck down there by a

musket-ball, and——Troops have proceeded. Will
arrive in half a minute after this." Mother aban-
dons all hope ; general commiseration ; troops rush
in, down a platform ; son only wounded, and em-
braces her.

As I have said, and as you will see, this is available for any purpose. But done with equal distinction and rapidity, it is a tremendous effect, and
got by the simplest means in the world. There is
nothing in the piece, but it was impossible not to
be moved and excited by the telegraph part of it.

I hope you have seen something of Stanny, and
have been to pantomimes with him, and have drunk
to the absent Dick. I miss you, my dear old boy,
at the play, woefully, and miss the walk home, and
the partings at the corner of Tavistock Square.
And when I go by myself, I come home stewing
Little Dorrit in my head ; and the best part of *my*
play is (or ought to be) in Gordon Street.

.   .   .   .   .   .

Ever affectionately.

[TO MR. W. WILKIE COLLINS]

49 Champs Élysées, Saturday, Jan. 19th, 1856.

My dear Collins :

I had no idea you were so far on with your book,
and heartily congratulate you on being within sight
of land.

It is excessively pleasant to me to get your letter, as it opens a perspective of theatrical and other lounging evenings, and also of articles in *Household Words*. It will not be the first time that we shall have got on well in Paris, and I hope it will not be by many a time the last.

I purpose coming over, early in February (as soon, in fact, as I shall have knocked out No. 5 of *Little D.*), and therefore we can return in a jovial manner together. As soon as I know my day of coming over, I will write to you again, and (as the merchants—say Charley—would add) "communicate same" to you.

The lodging, *en garçon*, shall be duly looked up, and I shall of course make a point of finding it close here. There will be no difficulty in that. I will have concluded the treaty before starting for London, and will take it by the month, both because that is the cheapest way, and because desirable places don't let for shorter terms.

I have been sitting to Scheffer to-day—conceive this, if you please, with No. 5 upon my soul—four hours!! I am so addleheaded and bored, that if you were here, I should propose an instantaneous rush to the Trois Frères. Under existing circumstances I have no consolation. . . . I met Madame Georges Sand the other day at a dinner got up by Madame Viardot for that great purpose. The

human mind cannot conceive any one more astonishingly opposed to all my preconceptions. If I had
been shown her in a state of repose, and asked what
I thought her to be, I should have said: "The
Queen's monthly nurse." *Au reste*, she has nothing
of the *bas bleu* about her, and is very quiet and
agreeable.

.   .   .   .   .   .

All unite in kindest remembrances to you, your
mother and brother.

Ever cordially.

[TO MR. W. WILKIE COLLINS]

TAVISTOCK HOUSE, June 6th, 1856.

My dear Collins :

I have never seen anything about myself in print
which has much correctness in it—any biographical account of myself I mean. I do not supply
such particulars when I am asked for them by editors and compilers, simply because I am asked for
them every day. If you want to prime Forgues,
you may tell him without fear of anything wrong,
that I was born at Portsmouth on the 7th of February, 1812; that my father was in the Navy Pay
Office; that I was taken by him to Chatham when
I was very young, and lived and was educated there
till I was twelve or thirteen, I suppose; that I was
then put to a school near London, where (as at

other places) I distinguished myself like a brick;
that I was put in the office of a solicitor, a friend of
my father's, and didn't much like it; and after a
couple of years (as well as I can remember) applied
myself with a celestial or diabolical energy to the
study of such things as would qualify me to be a
first-rate parliamentary reporter—at that time a
calling pursued by many clever men who were
young at the Bar; that I made my début in the
gallery (at about eighteen, I suppose), engaged on
a voluminous publication no longer in existence,
called *The Mirror of Parliament ;* that when *The
Morning Chronicle* was purchased by Sir John East-
hope and acquired a large circulation, I was engaged there, and that I remained there until I had
begun to publish *Pickwick*, when I found myself
in a condition to relinquish that part of my la-
bours; that I left the reputation behind me of
being the best and most rapid reporter ever known,
and that I could do anything in that way under any
sort of circumstances, and often did. (I daresay I
am at this present writing the best shorthand writer
in the world.)

   That I began, without any interest or introduction of any kind, to write fugitive pieces for the old
Monthly Magazine, when I was in the gallery for
The Mirror of Parliament ; that my faculty for descriptive writing was seized upon the moment I

joined *The Morning Chronicle*, and that I was liberally paid there and handsomely acknowledged, and wrote the greater part of the short descriptive *Sketches by Boz* in that paper; that I had been a writer when I was a mere baby, and always an actor from the same age; that I married the daughter of a writer to the signet in Edinburgh, who was the great friend and assistant of Scott, and who first made Lockhart known to him.

And that here I am.

Finally, if you want any dates of publication of books, tell Wills and he'll get them for you.

This is the first time I ever set down even these particulars, and, glancing them over, I feel like a wild beast in a caravan describing himself in the keeper's absence.

Ever faithfully.

P.S.—I made a speech last night at the London Tavern, at the end of which all the company sat holding their napkins to their eyes with one hand, and putting the other into their pockets. A hundred people or so contributed nine hundred pounds then and there.

[TO MR. WASHINGTON IRVING]

TAVISTOCK HOUSE, LONDON, July 5th, 1856.

My dear Irving :

. . . . .

Holland House has four - and - twenty youthful pages in it now—twelve for my lord, and twelve for my lady ; and no clergyman coils his leg up under his chair all dinner-time, and begins to uncurve it when the hostess goes. No wheeled chair runs smoothly in with that beaming face in it ; and ——'s little cotton pocket-handkerchief helped to make (I believe) this very sheet of paper. A half-sad, half-ludicrous story of Rogers is all I will sully it with. You know, I daresay, that for a year or so before his death he wandered, and lost himself like one of the Children in the Wood, grown up there and grown down again. He had Mrs. Procter and Mrs. Carlyle to breakfast with him one morning— only those two. Both excessively talkative, very quick and clever, and bent on entertaining him. When Mrs. Carlyle had flashed and shone before him for about three-quarters of an hour on one subject, he turned his poor old eyes on Mrs. Procter, and pointing to the brilliant discourser with his poor old finger, said (indignantly), " Who is *she ?* " Upon this, Mrs. Procter, cutting in, delivered (it is her own story) a neat oration on the life and writ-

ings of Carlyle, and enlightened him in her happiest
and airiest manner ; all of which he heard, staring
in the dreariest silence, and then said (indignantly
as before), "And who are *you ?* "

Ever, my dear Irving,

Most affectionately and truly yours.

[TO M. DE CERJAT]

TAVISTOCK HOUSE, Monday Night, Jan. 17th, 1857.

My dear Cerjat :

.   .   .   .   .   .

Down at Gad's Hill, near Rochester, in Kent—
Shakespeare's Gad's Hill, where Falstaff engaged in
the robbery—is a quaint little country-house of
Queen Anne's time. I happened to be walking
past, a year and a half or so ago, with my sub-
editor of *Household Words*, when I said to him :
"You see that house? It has always a curious
interest for me, because when I was a small boy
down in these parts I thought it the most beautiful
house (I suppose because of its famous old cedar-
trees) ever seen. And my poor father used to
bring me to look at it, and used to say that if ever
I grew up to be a clever man perhaps I might own
that house, or such another house. In remembrance of which, I have always in passing looked to
see if it was to be sold or let, and it has never been

to me like any other house, and it has never changed at all." We came back to town, and my friend went out to dinner. Next morning he came to me in great excitement, and said : "It is written that you were to have that house at Gad's Hill. The lady I had allotted to me to take down to dinner yesterday began to speak of that neighborhood. 'You know it?' I said ; 'I have been there to-day.' 'O yes,' said she, 'I know it very well. I was a child there, in the house they call Gad's Hill Place. My father was the rector, and lived there many years. He has just died, has left it to me, and I want to sell it.' 'So,' says the sub-editor, 'you must buy it. Now or never.'" I did, and hope to pass next summer there, though I may, perhaps, let it afterwards, furnished, from time to time.

. . . . . .

Adieu, my dear fellow ; ever cordially yours.

[TO MR. FRANK STONE, A.R.A.]

OFFICE OF "HOUSEHOLD WORDS," Monday, June 1st, 1857.

My dear Stone :

I know that what I am going to say will not be agreeable ; but I rely on the authoress's good sense ; and say it, knowing it to be the truth.

These *Notes* are destroyed by too much smartness. It gives the appearance of perpetual effort, stabs to the heart the nature that is in them, and wearies by the manner and not by the matter. It is the commonest fault in the world (as I have constant occasion to observe here), but it is a very great one. Just as you couldn't bear to have an épergne or a candlestick on your table, supported by a light figure always on tiptoe and evidently in an impossible attitude for the sustainment of its weight, so all readers would be more or less oppressed and worried by this presentation of everything in one smart point of view, when they know it must have other, and weightier, and more solid properties. Airiness and good spirits are always delightful, and are inseparable from notes of a cheerful trip ; but they should sympathise with many things as well as see them in a lively way. It is but a word or a touch that expresses this humanity, but without that little embellishment of good nature there is no such thing as humour. In this little MS. everything is too much patronised and condescended to, whereas the slightest touch of feeling for the rustic who is of the earth earthy, or of sisterhood with the homely servant who has made her face shine in her desire to please, would make a difference that the writer can scarcely imagine without trying it. The only relief in the twenty-one slips is the little bit about the chimes.

It *is* a relief, simply because it is an indication of some kind of sentiment. You don't want any sentiment laboriously made out in such a thing. You don't want any maudlin show of it. But you do want a pervading suggestion that it is there. It makes all the difference between being playful and being cruel. Again I must say, above all things—especially to young people writing : For the love of God, don't condescend ! Don't assume the attitude of saying, " See how clever I am, and what fun everybody else is !" Take any shape but that.

I observe an excellent quality of observation throughout, and think the boy at the shop, and all about him, particularly good. I have no doubt whatever that the rest of the journal will be much better if the writer chooses to make it so. If she considers for a moment within herself, she will know that she derived pleasure from everything she saw, because she saw it with innumerable lights and shades upon it, and bound to humanity by innumerable fine links ; she cannot possibly communicate anything of that pleasure to another by showing it from one little limited point only, and that point, observe, the one from which it is impossible to detach the exponent as the patroness of a whole universe of inferior souls. This is what everybody would mean in objecting to these notes (supposing them to be published), that they are too smart and too flippant.

As I understand this matter to be altogether between us three, and as I think your confidence, and her's, imposes a duty of friendship on me, I discharge it to the best of my ability. Perhaps I make more of it than you may have meant or expected ; if so, it is because I am interested and wish to express it. If there had been anything in my objection not perfectly easy of removal, I might, after all, have hesitated to state it ; but that is not the case. A very little indeed would make all this gaiety as sound and wholesome and good-natured in the reader's mind as it is in the writer's.

Affectionately always.

[TO MR. EDMUND YATES]

TAVISTOCK HOUSE, Tuesday, Feb. 2d, 1858.

My dear Yates :

Your quotation is, as I supposed, all wrong. The text is *not* "which his 'owls was organs." When Mr. Harris went into an empty dog-kennel, to spare his sensitive nature the anguish of overhearing Mrs. Harris's exclamations on the occasion of the birth of her first child (the Princess Royal of the Harris family), "he never took his hands away from his ears, or came out once, till he was showed the

baby." On encountering that spectacle, he was
(being of a weakly constitution) "took with fits."
For this distressing complaint he was medically
treated; the doctor "collared him, and laid him on
his back upon the airy stones"—please to observe
what follows—"and she was told, to ease her mind,
his 'owls was organs."

That is to say, Mrs. Harris, lying exhausted on
her bed, in the first sweet relief of freedom from
pain, merely covered with the counterpane, and not
yet "put comfortable," hears a noise apparently
proceeding from the back-yard, and says, in a
flushed and hysterical manner: "What 'owls are
those? Who is a-'owling? Not my ugebond?"
Upon which the doctor, looking round one of the
bottom posts of the bed, and taking Mrs. Harris's
pulse in a reassuring manner, says, with much
admirable presence of mind: "Howls, my dear
madam?—no, no, no! What are we thinking of?
Howls, my dear Mrs. Harris? Ha, ha, ha! Organs,
ma'am, organs. Organs in the streets, Mrs. Harris;
no howls."

Yours faithfully.

[TO MR. JOHN FORSTER]

TAVISTOCK HOUSE, Wednesday Night, Feb. 3d, 1858.

My dear Forster :

I beg to report two phenomena :

1. An excellent little play in one act, by Marston, at the Lyceum ; title, *A Hard Struggle ;* as good as *La Joie fait Peur,* though not at all like it.

2. Capital acting in the same play, by Mr. Dillon. Real good acting, in imitation of nobody, and honestly made out by himself ! !

I went (at Marston's request) last night, and cried till I sobbed again. I have not seen a word about it from Oxenford. But it is as wholesome and manly a thing altogether as I have seen for many a day. (I would have given a hundred pounds to have played Mr. Dillon's part.)

Love to Mrs. Forster.

Ever affectionately.

[TO DR. WESTLAND MARSTON]

TAVISTOCK HOUSE, Wednesday, Feb. 3d, 1858.

My dear Marston :

I most heartily and honestly congratulate you on your charming little piece. It moved me more than I could easily tell you, if I were to try. Except

La Joie fait Peur, I have seen nothing nearly so
good, and there is a subtlety in the comfortable
presentation of the child who is to become a devoted
woman for Reuben's sake, which goes a long way
beyond Madame de Girardin. I am at a loss to let
you know how much I admired it last night, or how
heartily I cried over it. A touching idea, most delicately conceived and wrought out by a true artist
and poet, in a spirit of noble, manly generosity, that
no one should be able to study without great
emotion.

It is extremely well acted by all concerned ; but
Mr. Dillon's performance is really admirable, and
deserving of the highest commendation. It is good
in these days to see an actor taking such pains, and
expressing such natural and vigorous sentiment.
There is only one thing I should have liked him to
change. I am much mistaken if any man—least of
all any such man—would crush a letter written by
the hand of the woman he loved. Hold it to his
heart unconsciously and look about for it the while,
he might ; or he might do any other thing with
it that expressed a habit of tenderness and affection
in association with the idea of her ; but he would
never crush it under any circumstances. He would
as soon crush her heart.

You will see how closely I went with him, by my
minding so slight an incident in so fine a perform-

9

ance. There is no one who could approach him in it; and I am bound to add that he surprised me as much as he pleased me.

I think it might be worth while to try the people at the Français with the piece. They are very good in one-act plays; such plays take well there, and this seems to me well suited to them. If you would like Samson or Regnier to read the play (in English), I know them well, and would be very glad indeed to tell them that I sent it with your sanction because I had been so much struck by it.

Faithfully yours always.

[TO MONSIEUR REGNIER]

TAVISTOCK HOUSE, LONDON, W. C., Thursday, Feb. 11th, 1858.

My dear Regnier :

I want you to read the enclosed little play. You will see that it is in one act—about the length of *La Joie fait Peur.* It is now acting at the Lyceum Theatre here, with very great success. The author is Mr. Westland Marston, a dramatic writer of reputation, who wrote a very well-known tragedy called *The Patrician's Daughter*, in which Macready and Miss Faucit acted (under Macready's management at Drury Lane) some years ago.

This little piece is so very powerful on the stage, its interest is so simple and natural, and the part of

Reuben is such a very fine one, that I cannot help thinking you might make one grand *coup* with it, if with your skilful hand you arranged it for the Français. I have communicated this idea of mine to the author, "*et là-dessus je vous écris.*" I am anxious to know your opinion, and shall expect with much interest to receive a little letter from you at your convenience.

Mrs. Dickens, Miss Hogarth, and all the house send a thousand kind loves and regards to Madame Regnier and the dear little boys. You will bring them to London when you come, with all the force of the Français—will you not?

Ever, my dear Regnier, faithfully your Friend.

[TO MR. EDMUND YATES]

TAVISTOCK HOUSE, TAVISTOCK SQUARE, LONDON, W. C.,
Wednesday, April 28th, 1858.

My dear Yates :

For a good many years I have suffered a great deal from charities, but never anything like what I suffer now. The amount of correspondence they inflict upon me is really incredible. But this is nothing. Benevolent men get behind the piers of the gates, lying in wait for my going out; and when I peep shrinkingly from my study-windows, I see their pot-bellied shadows projected on the gravel.

Benevolent bullies drive up in hansom cabs (with engraved portraits of their benevolent institutions hanging over the aprons, like banners on their outward walls), and stay long at the door. Benevolent area-sneaks get lost in the kitchens and are found to impede the circulation of the knife-cleaning machine. My man has been heard to say (at The Burton Arms) "that if it was a wicious place, well and good—*that* an't door work; but that wen all the Christian wirtues is always a-shoulderin' and a-helberin' on you in the 'all, a-tryin' to git past you and cut upstairs into master's room, why no wages as you couldn't name wouldn't make it up to you."

Persecuted ever.

[TO MISS HOGARTH]

MORRISON'S HOTEL, DUBLIN, Wednesday, Aug. 25th, 1858.

.   .   .   .   .   .

They were a highly excitable audience last night, but they certainly did not comprehend—internally and intellectually comprehend—*The Chimes* as a London audience do. I am quite sure of it. I very much doubt the Irish capacity of receiving the pathetic; but of their quickness as to the humorous there can be no doubt. I shall see how they go along with Little Paul, in his death, presently.

While I was at breakfast this morning, a general

officer was announced with great state—having a staff at the door—and came in, booted and plumed, and covered with Crimean decorations. It was Cunninghame, whom we knew in Genoa—then a captain. He was very hearty indeed, and came to ask me to dinner. Of course I couldn't go. Olliffe has a brother at Cork, who has just now (noon) written to me, proposing dinners and excursions in that neighbourhood which would fill about a week; I being there a day and a half, and reading three times. The work will be very severe here, and I begin to feel depressed by it. (By "here," I mean Ireland generally, please to observe.)

We meant, as I said in a letter to Katie, to go to Queenstown yesterday and bask on the seashore. But there is always so much to do that we couldn't manage it after all. We expect a tremendous house to-morrow night as well as to-day; and Arthur is at the present instant up to his eyes in business (and seats), and, between his regret at losing to-night, and his desire to make the room hold twice as many as it *will* hold, is half distracted. I have become a wonderful Irishman—must play an Irish part some day—and his only relaxation is when I enact "John and the Boots," which I consequently do enact all day long. The papers are full of remarks upon my white tie, and describe it as being of enormous size, which is a wonderful delusion, because, as you very well know, it is a small tie. Generally, I am happy to report, the Emerald press is in favour of my appearance, and likes my eyes. But one gentleman comes out with a letter at Cork, wherein he says that although only forty-six I look like an old man. *He* is a rum customer, I think.

The Rutherfords are living here, and wanted me to dine with them, which, I needn't say, could not be done; all manner of people have called, but I have seen only two. John has given it up altogether as to rivalry with the Boots, and did not come into my room this morning at all. Boots appeared triumphant and alone. He was waiting for me at the hotel-door last night. " Whaa't sart of a hoose, sur?" he asked me. "Capital." "The Lard be praised for the 'onor o' Dooblin!"

Arthur buys bad apples in the streets and brings them home and doesn't eat them, and then I am obliged to put them in the balcony because they make the room smell faint. Also he meets countrymen with honeycomb on their heads, and leads them (by the buttonhole when they have one) to this gorgeous establishment and requests the bar to buy honeycomb for his breakfast; then it stands upon the sideboard uncovered and the flies fall into it. He buys owls, too, and castles, and other horrible objects, made in bog-oak (that material which is not appreciated at Gad's Hill); and he is perpetually snipping pieces out of newspapers and sending them all over the world. While I am reading he conducts the correspondence, and his great delight is to show me seventeen or eighteen letters when I come, exhausted, into the retiring-place. Berry has not got into any particular trouble for forty-eight hours, except that he is all over boils. I have pre-scribed yeast, but ineffectually. It is indeed a sight to see him and John sitting in pay-boxes, and sur-veying Ireland out of pigeon-holes.

Same Evening before Bed-time.

.   .   .   .   .   .

Here follows a dialogue (but it requires imita-tion), which I had yesterday morning with a little boy of the house—landlord's son, I suppose—about Plorn's age. I am sitting on the sofa writing, and find him sitting beside me.

INIMITABLE. Holloa, old chap.

YOUNG IRELAND. Hal-loo!

INIMITABLE (*in his delightful way*). What a nice old fel-low you are. I am very fond of little boys.

YOUNG IRELAND. Air ye ? Ye'r right.

INIMITABLE. What do you learn, old fellow ?

YOUNG IRELAND (*very intent on Inimitable, and always childish, except in his brogue*). I lairn wureds of three sillibils, and wureds of two sillibils, and wureds of one sillibil.

INIMITABLE (*gaily*). Get out, you humbug ! You learn only words of one syllable.

YOUNG IRELAND (*laughs heartily*).   You may say that it is mostly wureds of one sillibil.

INIMITABLE.   Can you write ?

YOUNG IRELAND.   Not yet.   Things comes by deegrays.

INIMITABLE.   Can you cipher ?

YOUNG IRELAND (*very quickly*).   Wha'at's that ?

INIMITABLE.   Can you make figures ?

YOUNG IRELAND.   I can make a nought, which is not asy, being roond.

INIMITABLE.   I say, old boy, wasn't it you I saw on Sunday morning in the hall, in a soldier's cap ?   You know—in a soldier's cap ?

YOUNG IRELAND (*cogitating deeply*).   Was it a very good cap ?

INIMITABLE.   Yes.

YOUNG IRELAND.   Did it fit unkommon ?

INIMITABLE.   Yes.

YOUNG IRELAND.   Dat was me !

There are two stupid old louts at the room, to show people into their places, whom John calls "them two old Paddies," and of whom he says, that he "never see nothing like them (snigger) hold idiots" (snigger).   They bow and walk backwards before the grandees, and our men hustle them while they are doing it.

.   .   .   .

Ever, my dearest Georgy, most affectionately.

[TO MISS DICKENS]

BELFAST, Saturday, Aug. 28th, 1858.

When I went down to the Rotunda at Dublin on
Thursday night, I said to Arthur, who came rush-
ing at me: "You needn't tell me. I know all about
it." The moment I had come out of the door of
the hotel (a mile off), I had come against the stream
of people turned away. I had struggled against it
to the room. There, the crowd in all the lobbies
and passages was so great, that I had a difficulty
in getting in. They had broken all the glass in
the pay-boxes. They had offered frantic prices
for stalls. Eleven bank-notes were thrust into
that pay-box (Arthur saw them) at one time, for
eleven stalls. Our men were flattened against
walls, and squeezed against beams. Ladies stood
all night with their chins against my platform.
Other ladies sat all night upon my steps. You
never saw such a sight. And the reading went
tremendously! It is much to be regretted that we
troubled ourselves to go anywhere else in Ireland.
We turned away people enough to make immense
houses for a week. ˙

  ·   ·   ·   ·   ·   ·

Our men are rather indignant with the Irish
crowds, because in the struggle they don't sell

books, and because, in the pressure, they can't force a way into the room afterwards to sell them. They are deeply interested in the success, however, and are as zealous and ardent as possible. I shall write to Katie next. Give her my best love, and kiss the darling Plorn for me, and give my love to all the boys.

Ever, my dearest Mamie,
Your most affectionate Father.

[TO MISS HOGARTH]

MORRISON'S HOTEL, DUBLIN, Sunday Night, Aug. 29th, 1858.

I am so delighted to find your letter here to-night (eleven o'clock), and so afraid that, in the wear and tear of this strange life, I have written to Gad's Hill in the wrong order, and have not written to you, as I should, that I resolve to write this before going to bed. You will find it a wretchedly stupid letter; but you may imagine, my dearest girl, that I am tired.

The success at Belfast has been equal to the success here. Enormous! We turned away half the town. I think them a better audience, on the whole, than Dublin; and the personal affection there was something overwhelming. I wish you and the dear girls could have seen the people look

at me in the street; or heard them ask me, as I
hurried to the hotel after reading last night, to
"do me the honour to shake hands, Misther Dickens, and God bless you, sir; not ounly for the light
you've been to me this night, but for the light
you've been in mee house, sir (and God love your
face), this many a year." Every night, by-the-bye,
since I have been in Ireland, the ladies have beguiled John out of the bouquet from my coat. And
yesterday morning, as I had showered the leaves
from my geranium in reading "Little Dombey,"
they mounted the platform, after I was gone, and
picked them all up as keepsakes!

I have never seen *men* go in to cry so undisguisedly as they did at that reading yesterday
afternoon. They made no attempt whatever to
hide it, and certainly cried more than the women.
As to the "Boots" at night, and "Mrs. Gamp" too,
it was just one roar with me and them; for they
made me laugh so that sometimes I *could not* compose my face to go on.

You must not let the new idea of poor dear
Landor efface the former image of the fine old man.
I wouldn't blot him out, in his tender gallantry, as
he sat upon that bed at Forster's that night, for a
million of wild mistakes at eighty years of age.

I hope to be at Tavistock House before five
o'clock next Saturday morning, and to lie in bed

half the day, and come home by the 10.50 on Sunday.

. . . . . .

Ever affectionately.

[TO MISS HOGARTH]

ROYAL HOTEL, SCARBOROUGH, Sunday, Sept. 11th, 1858.

My dearest Georgy :

We had a very fine house indeed at York. All kinds of applications have been made for another reading there, and no doubt it would be exceedingly productive ; but it cannot be done. At Harrogate yesterday ; the queerest place, with the strangest people in it, leading the oddest lives of dancing, newspaper reading, and tables d'hôte.

. . . . . .

My dearest love, of course, to the dear girls, and to the noble Plorn. Apropos of children, there was one gentleman at the "Little Dombey" yesterday morning, who exhibited, or rather concealed, the profoundest grief. After crying a good deal without hiding it, he covered his face with both his hands, and laid it down on the back of the seat before him, and really shook with emotion. He was not in mourning, but I supposed him to have lost some child in old time. There was a remarkably good fellow of thirty or so, too, who found something so very ludicrous in "Toots," that he *could not* compose himself at all, but laughed until he sat wiping his eyes with his handkerchief. And when- ever he felt "Toots" coming again he began to laugh and wipe his eyes afresh, and when he came he gave a kind of cry, as if it were too much for him. It was uncommonly droll, and made me laugh heartily.

Ever, dear Georgy, your most affectionate.

[TO MR. JOHN FORSTER]

TAVISTOCK HOUSE, TAVISTOCK SQUARE, LONDON,
Sunday, Oct. 10th, 1858.

My dear Forster :

As to the truth of the readings, I cannot tell you what the demonstrations of personal regard and re- spect are. How the densest and most uncomforta- bly-packed crowd will be hushed in an instant when I show my face. How the youth of colleges, and the old men of business in the town, seem equally unable to get near enough to me when they cheer me away at night. How common people and gen- tlefolks will stop me in the streets and say : " Mr. Dickens, will you let me touch the hand that has filled my home with so many friends?" And if you saw the mothers, and fathers, and sisters, and brothers in mourning, who invariably come to "Lit- tle Dombey," and if you studied the wonderful expression of comfort and reliance with which they hang about me, as if I had been with them, all kindness and delicacy, at their own little deathbed, you would think it one of the strangest things in the world.

As to the mere effect, of course I don't go on doing the thing so often without carefully observing myself and the people too in every little thing, and without (in consequence) greatly improving in it.

At Aberdeen, we were crammed to the street twice in one day. At Perth (where I thought when I arrived there literally could be nobody to come), the nobility came posting in from thirty miles round, and the whole town came and filled an immense hall. As to the effect, if you had seen them after Lilian died, in *The Chimes*, or when Scrooge woke and talked to the boy outside the window, I doubt if you would ever have forgotten it. And at the end of "Dombey," yesterday afternoon, in the cold light of day, they all got up, after a short pause, gentle and simple, and thundered and waved their hats with that astonishing heartiness and fondness for me, that for the first time in all my public career they took me completely off my legs, and I saw the whole eighteen hundred of them reel on one side as if a shock from without had shaken the hall.

    •   •   •   •   •   •

Ever affectionately.

TAVISTOCK HOUSE, TAVISTOCK SQUARE, LONDON, W. C.,
Monday, Dec. 13th, 1858.

My dear Stone :

Many thanks for these discourses. They are
very good, I think, as expressing what many men
have felt and thought ; otherwise not specially remarkable. They have one fatal mistake, which is a
canker at the foot of their ever being widely useful.
Half the misery and hypocrisy of the Christian
world arises (as I take it) from a stubborn determination to refuse the New Testament as a sufficient guide in itself, and to force the Old Testament
into alliance with it—whereof comes all manner of
camel-swallowing and of gnat-straining. But so to
resent this miserable error, or to (by any implica-
tion) depreciate the divine goodness and beauty of
the New Testament, is to commit even a worse
error. And to class Jesus Christ with Mahomet is
simply audacity and folly. I might as well hoist
myself onto a high platform, to inform my disciples
that the lives of King George the Fourth and of
King Alfred the Great belonged to one and the
same category.

Ever affectionately.

[TO MR. ARTHUR SMITH]

TAVISTOCK HOUSE, TAVISTOCK SQUARE, LONDON, W.C.,
Wednesday, Jan. 26th, 1859.

My dear Arthur :
  Will you first read the enclosed letters, having
previously welcomed, with all possible cordiality,
the bearer, Mr. Thomas C. Evans, from New
York?

  You having read them, let me explain that Mr.
Fields is a highly respectable and influential man,
one of the heads of the most classical and most respected publishing house in America ; that Mr.
Richard Grant White is a man of high reputation ;
and that Felton is the Greek Professor in their
Cambridge University, perhaps the most distinguished scholar in the States.

  The address to myself, referred to in one of the
letters, being on its way, it is quite clear that I
must give some decided and definite answer to the
American proposal.   Now, will you carefully discuss it with Mr. Evans before I enter on it at all?
Then, will you dine here with him on Sunday—
which I will propose to him—and arrange to meet
at half-past four for an hour's discussion ?

  The points are these :

  First.   I have a very grave question within myself whether I could go to America at all.

Secondly. If I did go, I could not possibly go before the autumn.

Thirdly. If I did go, how long must I stay?

Fourthly. If the stay were a short one, could *you* go?

Fifthly. What is his project? What could I make? What occurs to you upon his proposal?

I have told him that the business arrangements of the readings have been from the first so entirely in your hands, that I enter upon nothing connected with them without previous reference to you.

Ever faithfully.

[TO M. DE CERJAT]

TAVISTOCK HOUSE, Tuesday, Feb. 1st, 1859.

My dear Cerjat :

.   .   .   .   .   .

My affairs domestic (which I know are not without their interest for you) flow peacefully. My eldest daughter is a capital housekeeper, heads the table gracefully, delegates certain appropriate duties to her sister and her aunt, and they are all three devotedly attached. Charley, my eldest boy, remains in Barings' house. Your present correspondent is more popular than he ever has been. I rather think that the readings in the country have opened up a new public who were outside before ;

10

but however that may be, his books have a wider
range than they ever had, and his public welcomes
are prodigious. Said correspondent is at present
overwhelmed with proposals to go and read in
America. Will never go, unless a small fortune
be first paid down in money on this side of the
Atlantic. Stated the figure of such payment, between ourselves, only yesterday. Expects to hear
no more of it, and assuredly will never go for less.
You don't say, my dear Cerjat, when you are coming to England! Somehow I feel that this mar-
riage ought to bring you over, though I don't know
why. You shall have a bed here and a bed at
Gad's Hill, and we will go and see strange sights
together. When I was in Ireland, I ordered the
brightest jaunting-car that ever was seen. It has
just this minute arrived per steamer from Belfast.
Say you are coming, and you shall be the first man
turned over by it; somebody must be (for my
daughter Mary drives anything that can be har-
nessed, and I know of no English horse that would
understand a jaunting-car coming down a Kentish
hill), and you shall be that somebody if you will.
They turned the basket-phaeton over, last summer,
in a bye-road—Mary and the other two—and had
to get it up again; which they did, and came home
as if nothing had happened. They send their loves
to Mrs. Cerjat, and to you, and to all, and particu-

larly to the dear *fiancée*. So do I, with all my heart, and am ever your attached and affectionate friend.

[TO MR. JOHN FORSTER]

GAD'S HILL, Thursday Night, Aug. 25th, 1859.

My dear Forster :

Heartily, glad to get your letter this morning.

I cannot easily tell you how much interested I am by what you tell me of our brave and excellent friend the Chief Baron, in connection with that ruffian. I followed the case with so much interest, and have followed the miserable knaves and asses who have perverted it since, with so much indignation, that I have often had more than half a mind to write and thank the upright judge who tried him. I declare to God that I believe such a service one of the greatest that a man of intellect and courage can render to society. Of course I saw the beast of a prisoner (with my mind's eye) delivering his cut-and-dried speech, and read in every word of it that no one but the murderer could have delivered or conceived it. Of course I have been driving the girls out of their wits here, by incessantly proclaiming that there needed no medical evidence either way, and that the case was plain without it. Lastly, of course (though a merciful man—because a merciful man I mean), I would hang any Home Secretary (Whig, Tory, Radical, or otherwise) who should step in between that black scoundrel and the gallows. I can*not* believe—and my belief in all wrong as to public matters is enormous—that such a thing will be done.

I am reminded of Tennyson, by thinking that King Arthur would have made short work of the amiable Smethurst, whom the newspapers strangely delight to call "Doctor," by-the-bye, and to make a sort of gentleman of. How fine the *Idylls* are ! Lord ! what a blessed thing it is to read a man who can write ! I thought nothing could be grander than the first poem till I came to the third ; but when I had read the last, it seemed to be absolutely unapproached and unapproachable.

    • • • • • •

Ever affectionately.

[TO MR. W. WILKIE COLLINS]

TAVISTOCK HOUSE, TAVISTOCK SQUARE, LONDON, W. C.,
Saturday Night, Jan. 7th, 1860.

My dear Wilkie :

I have read this book with great care and attention. There cannot be a doubt that it is a very great advance on all your former writing, and most especially in respect of tenderness. In character it is excellent. Mr. Fairlie as good as the lawyer, and

the lawyer as good as he. Mr. Vesey and Miss
Halcombe, in their different ways, equally meritorious. Sir Percival, also, is most skilfully shown,
though I doubt (you see what small points I come
to) whether any man ever showed uneasiness by
hand or foot without being forced by nature to
show it in his face too. The story is very interesting, and the writing of it admirable.

I seem to have noticed, here and there, that the
great pains you take express themselves a trifle too
much, and you know that I always contest your disposition to give an audience credit for nothing,
which necessarily involves the forcing of points on
their attention, and which I have always observed
them to resent when they find it out—as they
always will and do. But on turning to the book
again, I find it difficult to take out an instance of
this. It rather belongs to your habit of thought
and manner of going about the work. Perhaps I
express my meaning best when I say that the three
people who write the narratives in these proofs have
a DISSECTIVE property in common, which is essentially
not theirs but yours ; and that my own effort would
be to strike more of what is got *that way* out of them
by collision with one another, and by the working
of the story.

You know what an interest I have felt in your
powers from the beginning of our friendship, and

how very high I rate them? *I* know that this is an admirable book, and that it grips the difficulties of the weekly portion and throws them in masterly style. No one else could do it half so well. I have stopped in every chapter to notice some instance of ingenuity, or some happy turn of writing ; and I am absolutely certain that you never did half so well yourself.

So go on and prosper, and let me see some more, when you have enough (for your own satisfaction) to show me. I think of coming in to back you up if I can get an idea for my series of gossiping papers. One of these days, please God, we may do a story together ; I have very odd half-formed notions, in a mist, of something that might be done that way.

Ever affectionately.

[TO MR. HENRY F. CHORLEY [1]]

TAVISTOCK HOUSE, TAVISTOCK SQUARE, W. C.,
Friday Night, Feb. 3, 1860.

My dear Chorley :
I can most honestly assure you that I think *Roccabella* a very remarkable book indeed.

.   .   .   .   .   .

I am not quite with you as to the Italians. Your knowledge of the Italian character seems to me sur-

---

[1] Published in the *Autobiography, Memoir, and Letters of Henry Fothergill Chorley.* Compiled by H. G. Hewlett.

prisingly subtle and penetrating ; but I think we owe
it to those most unhappy men and their political
wretchedness to ask ourselves mercifully, whether
their faults are not essentially the faults of a people
long oppressed and priest-ridden ;—whether their
tendency to slink and conspire is not a tendency
that spies in every dress, from the triple crown to
a lousy head, have engendered in their ancestors
through generations? Again, like you, I shudder
at the distresses that come of these unavailing ris-
ings ; my blood runs hotter, as yours does, at the
thought of the leaders safe, and the instruments
perishing by hundreds ; yet what is to be done?
Their wrongs are so great that they *will* rise from
time to time somehow. It would be to doubt the
eternal providence of God to doubt that they will
rise successfully at last. Unavailing struggles
against a dominant tyranny precede all successful
turning against it. And is it not a little hard in us
Englishmen, whose forefathers have risen so often
and striven against so much, to look on, in our own
security, through microscopes, and detect the motes
in the brains of men driven mad? Think, if you
and I were Italians, and had grown from boyhood
to our present time, menaced in every day through
all these years by that infernal confessional, dun-
geons, and soldiers, could we be better than these
men? Should we be so good? I should not, I am

afraid, if I know myself. Such things would make
of me a moody, bloodthirsty, implacable man, who
would do anything for revenge ; and if I compromised the truth—put it at the worst, habitually—
where should I ever have had it before me ? In the
old Jesuits' college at Genoa, on the Chiaja at Naples,
in the churches of Rome, at the University of Padua,
on the Piazza San Marco at Venice, where ? And
the government is in all these places, and in all
Italian places. I have seen something of these men.
I have known Mazzini and Gallenga ; Manin was
tutor to my daughters in Paris ; I have had long
talks about scores of them with poor Ary Scheffer,
who was their best friend. I have gone back to
Italy after ten years, and found the best men I had
known there exiled or in jail. I believe they have
the faults you ascribe to them (nationally, not indi-
vidually), but I could not find it in my heart, remembering their miseries, to exhibit those faults
without referring them back to their causes. You
will forgive my writing this, because I write it
exactly as I write my cordial little tribute to the
high merits of your book. If it were not a living
reality to me, I should care nothing about this point
of disagreement ; but you are far too earnest a man,
and far too able a man, to be left unremonstrated
with by an admiring reader. You cannot write so
well without influencing many people. If you could

tell me that your book had but twenty readers, I
would reply, that so good a book will influence more
people's opinions, through those twenty, than a
worthless book would through twenty thousand;
and I express this with the perfect confidence of one
in whose mind the book has taken, for good and all,
a separate and distinct place.

Accept my thanks for the pleasure you have given
me. The poor acknowledgment of testifying to
that pleasure wherever I go will be my pleasure in
return. And so, my dear Chorley, good night, and
God bless you.

Ever faithfully yours.

[TO MR. JOHN FORSTER]

11, WELLINGTON STREET, NORTH STRAND, LONDON, W. C.,
Wednesday, May 2d, 1860.

My dear Forster :

It did not occur to me in reading your most excellent, interesting, and remarkable book, that[1] it
could with any reason be called one-sided. If Clarendon had never written his *History of the Re-
bellion*, then I can understand that it might be.
But just as it would be impossible to answer an
advocate who had misstated the merits of a case
for his own purpose, without, in the interests of
truth, and not of the other side merely, re-stating

[1] *The Impeachment of the Five Members.*

the merits and showing them in their real form, so
I cannot see the practicability of telling what you
had to tell without in some sort championing the
misrepresented side, and I think that you don't
do that as an advocate, but as a judge.

The evidence has been suppressed and coloured,
and the judge goes through it and puts it straight.
It is not *his* fault if it all goes one way and tends to
one plain conclusion. Nor is it his fault that it
goes the further when it is laid out straight, or
seems to do so, because it was so knotted and
twisted up before.

I can understand any man's, and particularly
Carlyle's, having a lingering respect that does not
like to be disturbed for those (in the best sense of
the word) loyal gentlemen of the country who went
with the king and were so true to him. But I
don't think Carlyle sufficiently considers that the
great mass of those gentlemen *didn't know the truth*,
that it was a part of their loyalty to believe what
they were told on the king's behalf, and that it is
reasonable to suppose that the king was too artful
to make known to *them* (especially after failure)
what were very acceptable designs to the desperate
soldiers of fortune about Whitehall. And it was to
me a curious point of adventitious interest arising
out of your book, to reflect on the probability of
their having been as ignorant of the real scheme in

Charles's head, as their descendants and followers down to this time, and to think with pity and admiration that they believed the cause to be so much better than it was. This is a notion I was anxious to have expressed in our account of the book in these pages. For I don't suppose Clarendon, or any other such man to sit down and tell posterity something that he has not "tried on" in his own time. Do you?

In the whole narrative I saw nothing anywhere to which I demurred. I admired it all, went with it all, and was proud of my friend's having written it all. I felt it to be all square and sound and right, and to be of enormous importance in these times. Firstly, to the people who (like myself) are so sick of the shortcomings of representative government as to have no interest in it. Secondly, to the humbugs at Westminster who have come down—a long, long way—from those men, as you know. When the great remonstrance came out, I was in the thick of my story, and was always busy with it ; but I am very glad I didn't read it then, as I shall read it now to much better purpose. All the time I was at work on the *Two Cities* I read no books but such as had the air of the time in them.

To return for a final word to the *Five Members*. I thought the marginal references overdone. Here and there, they had a comical look to me for that reason, and reminded me of shows and plays where everything is in the bill.

Lastly, I should have written to you—as I had a strong inclination to do, and ought to have done, immediately after reading the book—but for a weak reason ; of all things in the world I have lost heart in one—I hope no other—I cannot, times out calculation, make up my mind to write a letter.

Ever, my dear Forster, affectionately yours.

[TO SIR EDWARD BULWER LYTTON]

GAD'S HILL, Tuesday, June 5th, 1860.

My dear Bulwer Lytton :

I am very much interested and gratified by your letter concerning *A Tale of Two Cities.* I do not quite agree with you on two points, but that is no deduction from my pleasure.

In the first place, although the surrender of the feudal privileges (on a motion seconded by a nobleman of great rank) was the occasion of a sentimental scene, I see no reason to doubt, but on the contrary, many reasons to believe, that some of these privileges had been used to the frightful oppression of the peasant, quite as near to the time of the Revolution as the doctor's narrative, which, you will remember, dates long before the Terror. And surely when the new philosophy was the talk of the salons and the slang of the hour, it is not unreasonable or unallowable to suppose a nobleman wedded to the old cruel ideas, and representing the time going out, as his nephew represents the time coming in; as to the condition of the peasant in France generally at that day, I take it that if anything be certain on earth it is certain that it was intolerable. No *ex post facto* enquiries and provings by figures will hold water, surely, against the tremendous testimony of men living at the time.

There is a curious book printed at Amsterdam, written to make out no case whatever, and tiresome enough in its literal dictionary-like minuteness, scattered up and down the pages of which is full authority for my marquis. This is Mercier's *Tableau de Paris*. Rousseau is the authority for the peasant's shutting up his house when he had a bit of meat. The tax-taker was the authority for the wretched creature's impoverishment.

I am not clear, and I never have been clear, respecting that canon of fiction which forbids the interposition of accident in such a case as Madame Defarge's death. Where the accident is inseparable from the passion and emotion of the character, where it is strictly consistent with the whole design, and arises out of some culminating proceeding on the part of the character which the whole story has led up to, it seems to me to become, as it were, an act of divine justice. And when I use Miss Pross (though this is quite another question) to bring about that catastrophe, I have the positive intention of making that half-comic intervention a part of the desperate woman's failure, and of opposing that mean death—instead of a desperate one in the streets, which she wouldn't have minded—to the dignity of Carton's wrong or right ; this *was* the design, and seemed to be in the fitness of things.

.   .   .   .   .   .

Ever affectionately and faithfully.

[TO M. DE CERJAT]

OFFICE OF " ALL THE YEAR ROUND,"
Friday, Feb. 1st, 1861.

My dear Cerjat :

.   .   .   .   .   .

The American business is the greatest English sensation at present. I venture to predict that the struggle of violence will be a very short one, and will be soon succeeded by some new compact between the Northern and Southern States. Meantime the Lancashire mill-owners are getting very uneasy.

The Italian state of things is not regarded as looking very cheerful. What from one's natural sympathies with a people so oppressed as the Italians, and one's natural antagonism to a pope and a

Bourbon (both of which superstitions I do suppose the world to have had more than enough of), I agree with you concerning Victor Emmanuel, and greatly fear that the Southern Italians are much degraded. Still, an united Italy would be of vast importance to the peace of the world, and would be a rock in Louis Napoleon's way, as he very well knows. Therefore the idea must be championed, however much against hope.

.   .   .   .   .   .

This journal is doing gloriously, and *Great Expectations* is a great success. I have taken my third boy, Frank (Jeffrey's godson) into this office. If I am not mistaken, he has a natural literary taste and capacity, and may do very well with a chance so congenial to his mind, and being also entered at the Bar.

.   .   .   .   .   .

[TO MR. W. C. MACREADY] .

"ALL THE YEAR ROUND" OFFICE, Tuesday, June 11th, 1861.

My dearest Macready :

.   .   .   .   .   .

I have just finished my book of *Great Expectations*, and am the worse for wear. Neuralgic pains in the face have troubled me a good deal, and the work has been pretty close. But I hope that the book is a good book, and I have no doubt of very soon throwing off the little damage it has done me.

What with Blondin at the Crystal Palace and Leotard at Leicester Square, we seem to be going back to barbaric excitements. I have not seen, and don't intend to see, the Hero of Niagara (as the posters call him), but I have been beguiled into seeing Leotard, and it is at once the most fearful and most graceful thing I have ever seen done.

Clara White (grown pretty) has been staying with us.

I am sore afraid that *The Times*, by playing fast and loose with the American question, has very seriously compromised this country. The Americans northward are perfectly furious on the subject; and Motley the historian (a very sensible man, strongly English in his sympathies) assured me the other day that he thought the harm done very serious indeed, and the dangerous nature of the daily widening breach scarcely calculable.

Kindest and best love to all. Wilkie Collins has just come in, and sends best regard.

Ever most affectionately, my dearest Macready.

don addressed the crowd in the street. Fifty frantic men got up in all parts of the hall and addressed
me all at once. Other frantic men made speeches
to the walls. The whole Blackwood family were
borne in on the top of a wave, and landed with
their faces against the front of the platform. I
read with the platform crammed with people. I
got them to lie down upon it, and it was like some
impossible tableau or gigantic picnic; one pretty
girl in full dress lying on her side all night, holding
on to one of the legs of my table. It was the most
extraordinary sight. And yet from the moment I
began to the moment of my leaving off they never
missed a point, and they ended with a burst of
cheers.

. . . . . .

Give my love to Mamie. To her question, " Will
there be war with America?" I answer, "Yes;" I
fear the North to be utterly mad, and war to be un-
avoidable.

[TO MISS HOGARTH]

TORQUAY, Wednesday, Jan. 8th, 1862.

You know, I think, that I was very averse to
going to Plymouth, and would not have gone there
again but for poor Arthur. But on the last night
I read "Copperfield," and positively enthralled the
people. It was a most overpowering effect, and poor

Andrew [1] came behind the screen, after the storm,
and cried in the best and manliest manner. Also
there were two or three lines of his shipmates and
other sailors, and they were extraordinarily affected.
But its culminating effect was on Macready at
Cheltenham. When I got home after "Copperfield,"
I found him quite unable to speak, and able to
do nothing but square his dear old jaw all one
side, and roll his eyes (half closed), like Jackson's
picture of him. And when I said something
light about it, he returned : "No—er—Dickens !
I swear to Heaven that, as a piece of passion and
playfulness—er—indescribably mixed up together,
it does—er—no, really, Dickens !—amaze me as
profoundly as it moves me. But as a piece of art
—and you know—er—that I—no, Dickens ! By
—— ! have seen the best art in a great time—it is
incomprehensible to me. How is it got at—er—
how is it done—er—how one man can—well? It
lays me on my—er—back, and it is of no use talking
about it ! " With which he put his hand upon my
breast and pulled out his pocket-handkerchief, and
I felt as if I were doing somebody to his Werner.
Katie, by-the-bye, is a wonderful audience, and has
a great fund of wild feeling in her. Johnny not
at all unlike Plorn.

I have not yet seen the room here, but imagine it

[1] Lieutenant Andrew Gordon, R.N.

to be very small. Exeter I know, and that is small
also. I am very much used up, on the whole, for I
cannot bear this moist warm climate. It would
kill me very soon. And I have now got to the
point of taking so much out of myself with "Copperfield," that I might as well do Richard Wardour.

You have now, my dearest Georgy, the fullest extent of my tidings. This is a very pretty place—a
compound of Hastings, Tunbridge Wells, and little bits of the hills about Naples ; but I met four
respirators as I came up from the station, and three
pale curates without them, who seemed in a bad
way.

Frightful intelligence has just been brought in
by Boylett, concerning the small size of the room.
I have terrified Headland by sending him to look at
it, and swearing that if it's too small I will go away
to Exeter.

[TO M. DE CERJAT]

16, Hyde Park Gate, South Kensington Gore,
Sunday, March 16th, 1862.

My dear Cerjat :

.   .   .   .   .   .

You ask me about Fechter and his Hamlet. It
was a performance of extraordinary merit ; by far
the most coherent, consistent, and intelligible Hamlet I ever saw. Some of the delicacies with which

he rendered his conception clear were extremely subtle ; and in particular he avoided that brutality towards Ophelia which, with a greater or less amount of coarseness, I have seen in all other Hamlets. As a mere *tour de force*, it would have been very remarkable in its disclosure of a perfectly wonderful knowledge of the force of the English language ; but its merit was far beyond and above this. Foreign accent, of course, but not at all a disagreeable one. And he was so obviously safe and at ease, that you were never in pain for him as a foreigner. Add to this a perfectly picturesque and romantic " make up," and a remorseless destruction of all conventionalities, and you have the leading virtues of the impersonation. In Othello he did not succeed. In Iago he is very good. He is an admirable artist, and far beyond anyone on our stage. A real artist and a gentleman.

.   .   .   .   .

Yours affectionately.

[TO MISS DICKENS]

HôTEL DU HELDER, PARIS, Sunday, Feb. 1st, 1863.

My dearest Mamie :

I cannot give you any idea of the success of the readings here, because no one can imagine the scene of last Friday night at the Embassy. Such audiences and such enthusiasm I have never seen, but the thing culminated on Friday night in a two hours' storm of excitement and pleasure. They actually recommenced and applauded right away into their carriages and down the street.

You know your parent's horror of being lionised, and will not be surprised to hear that I am half dead of it. I cannot leave here until Thursday (though I am every hour in danger of running away) because I have to dine out, to say nothing of breakfasting—think of me breakfasting!—every intervening day. But my project is to send John home on Thursday, and then to go on a little perfectly quiet tour for about ten days, touching the sea at Boulogne. When I get there, I will write to your aunt (in case you should not be at home), saying when I shall arrive at the office. I must go to the office instead of Gad's, because I have much to do with Forster about Elliotson.

I enclose a short note for each of the little boys. Give Harry ten shillings pocket-money, and Plorn six.

The Olliffe girls, very nice. Florence at the readings, prodigiously excited.

My dearest Macready :

I have just come back from Paris, where the readings—" Copperfield," " Dombey " and " Trial," and
" Carol" and " Trial "—have made a sensation which
modesty (my natural modesty) renders it impossible
for me to describe. You know what a noble audience the Paris audience is ! They were at their
very noblest with me.

I was very much concerned by hearing hurriedly
from Georgy that you were ill. But when I came
home at night, she showed me Katie's letter, and
that set me up again. Ah, you have the best of
companions and nurses, and can afford to be ill
now and then for the happiness of being so brought
through it. But don't do it again yet awhile for
all that.

Legouvé (whom you remember in Paris as writing for the Ristori) was anxious that I should bring
you the enclosed. A manly and generous effort, I
think? Regnier desired to be warmly remembered to you. He looks just as of yore.

Paris generally is about as wicked and extrava-
gant as in the days of the Regency. Madame
Viardot in the *Orphée*, most splendid. An

opera of *Faust*, a very sad and noble rendering
of that sad and noble story. Stage management
remarkable for some admirable, and really poetical,
effects of light. In the more striking situations,
Mephistopheles surrounded by an infernal red atmosphere of his own. Marguerite by a pale blue
mournful light. The two never blending. After
Marguerite has taken the jewels placed in her way
in the garden, a weird evening draws on, and the
·bloom fades from the flowers, and the leaves of the
trees droop and lose their fresh green, and mournful shadows overhang her chamber window, which
was innocently bright and gay at first. I couldn't
bear it, and gave in completely.

Fechter doing wonders over the way here, with
a picturesque French drama. Miss Kate Terry,
in a small part in it, perfectly charming. You may
remember her making a noise, years ago, doing a
boy at an inn, in *The Courier of Lyons?* She
has a tender love-scene in this piece, which is a
really beautiful and artistic thing. I saw her do
it at about three in the morning of the day when
the theatre opened, surrounded by shavings and
carpenters, and (of course) with that inevitable
hammer going; and I told Fechter: "That is the
very best piece of womanly tenderness I have ever
seen on the stage, and you'll find that no audience can miss it." It is a comfort to add that it

was instantly seized upon, and is much talked of.

Stanfield was very ill for some months, then suddenly picked up, and is really rosy and jovial again. Going to see him when he was very despondent, I told him the story of Fechter's piece (then in rehearsal) with appropriate action; fighting a duel with the washing-stand, defying the bedstead, and saving the life of the sofa-cushion. This so kindled his old theatrical ardour, that I think he turned the corner on the spot.

With love to Mrs. Macready and Katie, and (be still my heart!) Benvenuta, and the exiled Johnny (not too attentive at school, I hope?), and the personally-unknown young Parr,

Ever, my dearest Macready, your most affectionate.

[TO M. DE CERJAT]

GAD'S HILL PLACE, HIGHAM BY ROCHESTER, KENT,
Thursday, May 28th, 1863.

My dear Cerjat :

I don't wonder at your finding it difficult to reconcile your mind to a French Hamlet ; but I assure you that Fechter's is a very remarkable performance perfectly consistent with itself (whether it be my particular Hamlet, or your particular Hamlet, or no), a coherent and intelligent whole, and done by a true artist. I have never seen, I think, an intelligent and clear view of the whole character so well sustained throughout; and there is a very captivating air of romance and picturesqueness added, which is quite new. Rely upon it, the public were right. The thing could not have been sustained by oddity; it would have perished upon that, very soon. As to the mere accent, there is far less drawback in that than you would suppose. For this reason, he obviously knows English so thoroughly that you feel he is safe. You are never in pain for him. This sense of ease is gained directly, and then you think very little more about it.

The Colenso and Jowett matter is a more difficult question, but here again I don't go with you. The position of the writers of *Essays and Reviews* is, that certain parts of the Old Testament have done their intended function in the education of the world *as it was;* but that mankind, like the individual man, is designed by the Almighty to have an infancy and a maturity, and that as it advances, the machinery of its education must advance too. For example: inasmuch as ever since there was a sun and there was vapour, there *must have* been a rainbow under certain conditions, so surely it would be better now to recognise that indisputable fact. Similarly, Joshua might command the sun to stand still, under the impression that it moved round the earth; but he could not possibly have inverted the relations of the earth and the sun, whatever his impressions were. Again, it is contended that the science of geology is quite as much a revelation to man, as books of an immense age and of (at the best) doubtful origin, and that your consideration of the latter must reasonably be influenced by the former. As I understand the importance of timely suggestions such as these, it is, that the Church should not gradually shock and lose the more thoughtful and logical of human minds; but should be so gently and considerately yielding as to retain them, and, through them, hundreds of thousands. This seems to me, as I understand the temper and tendency of the time, whether for good or evil, to be a very wise and necessary position. And as I understand the danger, it is not chargeable on those who take this ground, but on those who in reply call names and argue nothing. What these bishops and such-like say about revelation, in assuming it to be finished and done with, I can't in the least understand. Nothing is discovered without God's intention and assistance, and I suppose every new knowledge of His works that is conceded to man to be distinctly a revelation by which men are to guide themselves. Lastly, in the mere matter of religious doctrine and dog-

mas, these men (Protestants—protestors—succes-
sors of the men who protested against human judgment being set aside) talk and write as if they were
all settled by the direct act of Heaven ; not as if
they had been, as we know they were, a matter of
temporary accommodation and adjustment among
disputing mortals as fallible as you or I.

.   .   .   .   .   .
.

A very intelligent German friend of mine, just
home from America, maintains that the conscrip-
tion will succeed in the North, and that the war
will be indefinitely prolonged. *I* say "No," and
that however mad and villainous the North is, the
war will finish by reason of its not supplying soldiers. We shall see. The more they brag the more
I don't believe in them.

.   .   .   .   .   .

[TO MR. CHARLES READE]

OFFICE OF " ALL THE YEAR ROUND,"
Wednesday, Sept. 30th, 1863.

My dear Reade :
I *must* write you one line to say how interested
I am in your story, and to congratulate you upon
its admirable art and its surprising grace and
vigour.

And to hint my hope, at the same time, that you

will be able to find leisure for a little dash for the Christmas number. It would be a really great and true pleasure to me if you could.

Faithfully yours always.

[TO MR. W. H. WILLS]

GAD'S HILL, Sunday, Dec. 20th, 1863.

My dear Wills :

I am clear that you took my cold. Why didn't you do the thing completely, and take it away from me ? for it hangs by me still.

Will you tell Mrs. Linton that in looking over her admirable account (*most* admirable) of Mrs. Gordon's book, I have taken out the references to Lockhart, not because I in the least doubt their justice, but because I knew him and he liked me ; and because one bright day in Rome, I walked about with him for some hours when he was dying fast, and all the old faults had faded out of him, and the now ghost of the handsome man I had first known when Scott's daughter was at the head of his house, had little more to do with this world than she in her grave, or Scott in his, or small Hugh Littlejohn in his. Lockhart had been anxious to see me all the previous day (when I was away on the Campagna), and as we walked about I knew very well that *he* knew very well why. He talked of getting better, but I never saw him again. This makes me stay Mrs. Linton's hand, gentle as it is.

Mrs. Lirriper is indeed a most brilliant old lady. God bless her.

I am glad to hear of your being "haunted," and hope to increase your stock of such ghosts pretty liberally.

Ever faithfully.

[TO MR. W. WILKIE COLLINS]

GAD'S HILL, Monday, Jan. 24th, 1864.

My dear Wilkie :

.   .   .   .   .   .

The Christmas number has been the greatest success of all; has shot ahead of last year; has sold about two hundred and twenty thousand; and has made the name of Mrs. Lirriper so swiftly and domestically famous as never was. I had a very strong belief in her when I wrote about her, finding that she made a great effect upon me ; but she certainly has gone beyond my hopes. (Probably you know nothing about her? which is a very unpleasant consideration.) Of the new book, I have done the two first numbers, and am now beginning the third. It is a combination of drollery with romance which requires a great deal of pains and a perfect throwing away of points that might be amplified ; but I hope it is *very good.* I confess, in short, that I think it is. Strange to say, I felt at first quite dazed in getting back to the large canvas and the big brushes ; and even now, I have a sensation as of acting at the San Carlo after Tavistock House, which I could hardly have supposed would have come upon so old a stager.

You will have read about poor Thackeray's death —sudden, and yet not sudden, for he had long been alarmingly ill. At the solicitation of Mr. Smith and some of his friends, I have done what I would most gladly have excused myself from doing, if I felt I could—written a couple of pages about him in what was his own magazine.

[TO MR. MARCUS STONE]

57, GLOUCESTER PLACE, HYDE PARK,
Tuesday, Feb. 23d, 1864.

My dear Marcus:

I think the design for the cover *excellent*, and do not doubt its coming out to perfection. The slight alteration I am going to suggest originates in a business consideration not to be overlooked.

The word *Our* in the title must be out in the open like *Mutual Friend*, making the title three distinct large lines— *Our* as big as *Mutual Friend* This would give you too much design at the bottom. I would therefore take out the dustman, and put the Wegg and Boffin composition (which is capital) in its place. I don't want Mr. Inspector or the murder reward bill, because these points are sufficiently indicated in the river at the top. Therefore you can have an indication of the dustman in Mr. Inspector's place. Note, that the dustman's face should be droll, and not horrible. Twemlow's elbow will still go out of the frame as it does now, and the same with Lizzie's skirts on the opposite side. With these changes, work away !

Mrs. Boffin, as I judge of her from the sketch, " very good, indeed." I want Boffin's oddity, without being at all blinked, to be an oddity of a very honest kind, that people will like.

The doll's dressmaker is immensely better than she was. I think she should now come extremely well. A weird sharpness not without beauty is the thing I want.

Affectionately always.

[TO MR. EDMUND OLLIER]

"ALL THE YEAR ROUND" OFFICE, March, 1864.

.   .   .   .   .   .

I want the article on "Working Men's Clubs" to refer back to "The Poor Man and his Beer" in No. 1, and to maintain the principle involved in that effort.

12

it is *very good.* I confess, in short, that I think it is. Strange to say, I felt at first quite dazed in getting back to the large canvas and the big brushes; and even now, I have a sensation as of acting at the San Carlo after Tavistock House, which I could hardly have supposed would have come upon so old a stager.

You will have read about poor Thackeray's death —sudden, and yet not sudden, for he had long been alarmingly ill. At the solicitation of Mr. Smith and some of his friends, I have done what I would most gladly have excused myself from doing, if I felt I could—written a couple of pages about him in what was his own magazine.

[TO MR. MARCUS STONE]

57, GLOUCESTER PLACE, HYDE PARK,
Tuesday, Feb. 23d, 1864.

My dear Marcus:

I think the design for the cover *excellent,* and do not doubt its coming out to perfection. The slight alteration I am going to suggest originates in a business consideration not to be overlooked.

The word *Our* in the title must be out in the open like *Mutual Friend,* making the title three distinct large lines—*Our* as big as *Mutual Friend* This would give you too much design at the bottom. I

GAD'S HILL PLACE, HIGHAM BY ROCHESTER,
Tuesday, Oct. 25th, 1864.

My dear Cerjat :

. . . . . .

In London there is, as you see by the papers,
extraordinarily little news. At present the appre-
hension (rather less than it was thought) of a commercial crisis, and the trial of Müller next Thursday, are the two chief sensations. I hope that
gentleman will be hanged, and have hardly a doubt
of it, though croakers contrariwise are not wanting.
. . . As to the Church, my friend, I am sick of
it. The spectacles presented by the indecent
squabbles of priests of most denominations, and
the exemplary unfairness and rancour with which
they conduct their differences, utterly repel me.
And the idea of the Protestant establishment, in
the face of its own history, seeking to trample out
discussion and private judgment, is an enormity so
cool, that I wonder the Right Reverends, Very Reverends, and all other Reverends, who commit it,
can look in one another's faces without laughing,
as the old soothsayers did. Perhaps they can't and
don't. How our sublime and so-different Christian religion is to be administered in the future I
cannot pretend to say, but that the Church's hand

is at its own throat I am fully convinced. Here, more Popery, there, more Methodism—as many forms of consignment to eternal damnation as there are articles, and all in one forever quarrelling body —the Master of the New Testament put out of sight, and the rage and fury almost always turning on the letter of obscure parts of the Old Testament, which itself has been the subject of accommodation, adaptation, varying interpretation without end— these things cannot last. The Church that is to have its part in the coming time must be a more Christian one, with less arbitrary pretensions and a stronger hold upon the mantle of our Saviour, as He walked and talked upon this earth.

Of family intelligence I have very little. Charles Collins continuing in a very poor way, and showing no signs of amendment. He and my daughter Katie went to Wiesbaden and thence to Nice, where they are now. I have strong apprehensions that he will never recover, and that she will be left a young widow. All the rest are as they were. Mary neither married nor going to be ; Georgina holding them all together and perpetually corresponding with the distant ones; occasional rallyings coming off here, in which another generation begins to peep above the table. I once used to think what a horrible thing it was to be a grandfather. Finding that the calamity falls upon me

without my perceiving any other change in myself,
I bear it like a man.

.   .   .   .   .   .

Affectionately yours.

[TO MR. THOMAS MITTON]

GAD'S HILL PLACE, HIGHAM BY ROCHESTER, KENT,
Tuesday, June 13th, 1865.

My dear Mitton :

I should have written to you yesterday or the
day before, if I had been quite up to writing.

I was in the only carriage that did not go over
into the stream. It was caught upon the turn by
some of the ruin of the bridge, and hung suspended
and balanced in an apparently impossible manner.
Two ladies were my fellow-passengers, an old one
and a young one. This is exactly what passed.
You may judge from it the precise length of the
suspense : Suddenly we were off the rail, and beat-
ing the ground as the car of a half-emptied balloon
might. The old lady cried out, " My God ! " and
the young one screamed. I caught hold of them
both (the old lady sat opposite and the young one
on my left), and said : " We can't help ourselves,
but we can be quiet and composed. Pray don't
cry out." The old lady immediately answered :
" Thank you. Rely upon me. Upon my soul I

will be quiet." We were all tilted down together in a corner of the carriage, and stopped. I said to them thereupon : "You may be sure nothing worse can happen. Our danger *must* be over. Will you remain here without stirring, while I get out of the window?" They both answered quite collectedly, "Yes," and I got out without the least notion what had happened. Fortunately I got out with great caution and stood upon the step. Looking down I saw the bridge gone, and nothing below me but the line of rail. Some people in the two other compartments were madly trying to plunge out at window, and had no idea that there was an open swampy field fifteen feet down below them, and nothing else! The two guards (one with his face cut) were running up and down on the down side of the bridge (which was not torn up) quite wildly. I called out to them : "Look at me. Do stop an instant and look at me, and tell me whether you don't know me." One of them answered : "We know you very well, Mr. Dickens." "Then," I said, "my good fellow, for God's sake give me your key, and send one of those labourers here, and I'll empty this carriage." We did it quite safely, by means of a plank or two, and when it was done I saw all the rest of the train, except the two baggage vans, down in the stream. I got into the carriage again for my brandy flask, took off my travelling hat for a basin, climbed down the brickwork, and filled my hat with water.

Suddenly I came upon a staggering man covered with blood (I think he must have been flung clean out of his carriage), with such a frightful cut across the skull that I couldn't bear to look at him. I poured some water over his face and gave him some to drink, then gave him some brandy, and laid him down on the grass, and he said, "I am gone," and died afterwards. Then I stumbled over a lady lying on her back against a little pollard-tree, with the blood streaming over her face (which was lead colour) in a number of distinct little streams from the head. I asked her if she could swallow a little brandy and she just nodded, and I gave her some and left her for somebody else. The next time I passed her she was dead. Then a man, examined at the inquest yesterday (who evidently had not the least remembrance of what really passed), came running up to me and implored me to help him find his wife, who was afterwards found dead. No imagination can conceive the ruin of the carriages, or the extraordinary weights under which the people were lying, or the complications into which they were twisted up among iron and wood, and mud and water.

I don't want to be examined at the inquest, and I don't want to write about it. I could do no good

either way, and I could only seem to speak about
myself, which, of course, I would rather not do. I
am keeping very quiet here. I have a—I don't
know what to call it—constitutional (I suppose)
presence of mind, and was not in the least fluttered
at the time. I instantly remembered that I had
the MS. of a number with me, and clambered back
into the carriage for it. But in writing these
scanty words of recollection I feel the shake and
am obliged to stop.

Ever faithfully.

[TO PROFESSOR OWEN, F.R.S.]

GAD'S HILL, Wednesday, July 12th, 1865.

My dear Owen :

Studying the gorilla last night for the twentieth
time, it suddenly came into my head that I had
never thanked you for that admirable treatise. This
is to bear witness to my blushes and repentance. If
you knew how much interest it has awakened in me,
and how often it has set me a-thinking, you would
consider me a more thankless beast than any gorilla
that ever lived. But happily you do *not* know, and
I am not going to tell you.

Believe me, ever faithfully yours.

[TO MRS. PROCTER]

GAD'S HILL PLACE, HIGHAM BY ROCHESTER, KENT,
Sept. 26th, 1865.

My dear Mrs. Procter :

I have written the little introduction,[1] and have sent it to my printer, in order that you may read it without trouble. But if you would like to keep the few pages of MS., of course they are yours.

It is brief, and I have aimed at perfect simplicity, and an avoidance of all that your beloved Adelaide would have wished avoided. Do not expect too much from it. If there should be anything wrong in fact, or anything that you would like changed for any reason, *of course you will tell me so*, and of course you will not deem it possible that you can trouble me by making any such request most freely.

You will probably receive the proof either on Friday or Saturday. Don't write to me until you have read it. In the meantime I send you back the two books, with the two letters in the bound one.

With love to Procter,

Ever your affectionate Friend.

[1] A preface to the collected poems of Adelaide Procter.

[TO M. DE CERJAT]

GAD'S HILL PLACE, HIGHAM BY ROCHESTER, KENT,
November 13th, 1865.

My dear Cerjat :

.   .   .   .   .   .

If the Americans don't embroil us in a war before long it will not be their fault. What with
their swagger and bombast, what with their claims
for indemnification, what with Ireland and Fenian-
ism, and what with Canada, I have strong apprehensions. With a settled animosity towards the
French usurper, I believe him to have always been
sound in his desire to divide the States against
themselves, and that we were unsound and wrong
in "letting I dare not wait upon I would." The
Jamaica insurrection is another hopeful piece of
business. That platform-sympathy with the black
—or the native, or the devil—afar off, and that
platform indifference to our own countrymen at
enormous odds in the midst of bloodshed and sav-
agery, makes me stark wild. Only the other day,
here was a meeting of jawbones of asses at Manchester, to censure the Jamaica Governor for his
manner of putting down the insurrection! So we
are badgered about New Zealanders and Hotten-
tots, as if they were identical with men in clean
shirts at Camberwell, and were to be bound by

pen and ink accordingly. So Exeter Hall holds us
in mortal submission to missionaries, who (Living-
stone always excepted) are perfect nuisances, and
leave every place worse than they found it.

Of all the many evidences that are visible of our
being ill-governed, no one is so remarkable to me
as our ignorance of what is going on under our
Government. What will future generations think
of that enormous Indian Mutiny being ripened
without suspicion, until whole regiments arose and
killed their officers? A week ago, red tape, half-
bouncing and half pooh-poohing what it bounced
at, would have scouted the idea of a Dublin jail not
being able to hold a political prisoner. But for the
blacks in Jamaica being over-impatient and before
their time, the whites might have been extermi-
nated, without a previous hint or suspicion that
there was anything amiss. *Laissez aller*, and Britons never, never, never !——

[TO MRS. BROOKFIELD]

OFFICE OF "ALL THE YEAR ROUND,"
Tuesday, Feb. 20th, 1866.

My dear Mrs. Brookfield :

Having gone through your MS. (which I should
have done sooner, but that I have not been very
well), I write these few following words about it.
Firstly, with a limited reference to its unsuitability

to these pages. Secondly, with a more enlarged
reference to the merits of the story itself.

If you will take any part of it and cut it up (in
fancy) into the small portions into which it would
have to be divided here for only a month's supply,
you will (I think) at once discover the impossibility
of publishing it in weekly parts. The scheme of
the chapters, the manner of introducing the people,
the progress of the interest, the places in which the
principal places fall, are all hopelessly against it.
It would seem as though the story were never coming, and hardly ever moving. There must be a special design to overcome that specially trying mode of
publication, and I cannot better express the difficulty and labour of it than by asking you to turn over
any two weekly numbers of *A Tale of Two Cities*, or
Great Expectations, or Bulwer's story, or Wilkie Collins's, or Reade's, or *At the Bar*, and notice how patiently and expressly the thing has to be planned for
presentation in these fragments, and yet for afterwards fusing together as an uninterrupted whole.

Of the story itself I honestly say that I think
highly. The style is particularly easy and agreeable, infinitely above ordinary writing, and sometimes reminds me of Mrs. Inchbald at her best.
The characters are remarkably well observed, and
with a rare mixture of delicacy and truthfulness. I
observe this particularly in the brother and sis-

ter, and in Mrs. Neville. But it strikes me that you constantly hurry your narrative (and yet without getting on) *by telling it, in a sort of impetuous breathless way, in your own person, when the people should tell it and act it for themselves.* My notion always is, that when I have made the people to play out the play, it is, as it were, their business to do it, and not mine. Then, unless you really have led up to a great situation like Basil's death, you are bound in art to make more of it. Such a scene should form a chapter of itself. Impressed upon the reader's memory, it would go far to make the fortune of the book. Suppose yourself telling that affecting incident in a letter to a friend. Wouldn't you describe how you went through the life and stir of the streets and roads to the sick-room? Wouldn't you say what kind of a room it was, what kind of day it was, whether it was sunlight, starlight, or moonlight? Wouldn't you have a strong impression on your mind of how you were received, when you first met the look of the dying man, what strange contrasts were about you and struck you? I don't want you, in a novel, to present *yourself*, to tell such things, but I want the things to be there. You make no more of the situation than the index might, or a descriptive playbill might in giving a summary of the tragedy under representation.

As a mere piece of mechanical workmanship, I

think all your chapters should be shorter; that is to say, that they should be subdivided. Also, when you change from narrative to dialogue, or *vice versâ*, you should make the transition more carefully. Also, taking the pains to sit down and recall the principal landmarks in your story, you should then make them far more elaborate and conspicuous than the rest. Even with these changes I do not believe that the story would attract the attention due to it, if it were published even in such monthly portions as the space of *Fraser* would admit of. Even so brightened, it would not, to the best of my judgment, express itself piecemeal. It seems to me to be so constituted as to require to be read " off the reel." As a book in two volumes I think it would have good claims to success, and good chances of obtaining success. But I suppose the polishing I have hinted at (not a meretricious adornment, but positively necessary to good work and good art) to have been first thoroughly administered.

Now don't hate me if you can help it. I can afford to be hated by some people, but I am not rich enough to put you in possession of that luxury.

Ever faithfully yours.

P.S.—The MS. shall be delivered at your house to-morrow. And your petitioner again prays not to be, etc.

[TO MR. B. W. PROCTER]

GAD'S HILL PLACE, HIGHAM BY ROCHESTER, KENT,
Monday, Aug. 13th, 1866.

My dear Procter :

I have read your biography of Charles Lamb with inexpressible pleasure and interest. I do not think it possible to tell a pathetic story with a more unaffected and manly tenderness. And as to the force and vigour of the style, if I did not know you I should have made sure that there was a printer's error in the opening of your introduction, and that the word " seventy " occupied the place of " forty."

Let me, my dear friend, most heartily congratulate you on your achievement. It is not an ordinary triumph to do such justice to the memory of such a man. And I venture to add, that the fresh spirit with which you have done it impresses me as being perfectly wonderful.

Ever affectionately yours.

[TO MR. W. C. MACREADY]

GAD'S HILL PLACE, HIGHAM BY ROCHESTER, KENT,
Friday, Dec. 28th, 1866.

My dearest Macready :

I have received your letter with the utmost pleasure and we all send our most affectionate love to you, Mrs. Macready, Katie, Johnny, and the boy of boys. All good Christmas and New Year greetings are to be understood as included.

You will be interested in knowing that, encouraged by the success of summer cricket-matches, I got up a quantity of foot-races and rustic sports in my field here on the 26th last past: as I have never yet had a case of drunkenness, the landlord of The Falstaff had a drinking-booth on the ground. All the prizes I gave were in money, too. We had two thousand people here. Among the crowd were soldiers, navvies, and labourers of all kinds. Not a stake was pulled up, or a rope slackened, or one farthing's-worth of damage done. To every competitor (only) a printed bill of general rules was given, with the concluding words: "Mr. Dickens puts every man upon his honour to assist in preserving order." There was not a dispute all day, and they went away at sunset rending the air with cheers, and leaving every flag on a six hundred yards' course as neat as they found it when the gates were opened at ten in the morning. Surely this is a bright sign in the neighbourhood of such a place as Chatham!

Mugby Junction turned, yesterday afternoon, the extraordinary number of two hundred and fifty thousand!

In the middle of next month I begin a new course of forty-two readings. If any of them bring me within reach of Cheltenham, with an hour to spare, I shall come on to you, even for that hour. More of this when I am afield and have my list, which Dolby (for Chappell) is now preparing.

Forster and Mrs. Forster were to have come to us next Monday, to stay until Saturday. I write "were," because I hear that Forster (who had a touch of bronchitis when he wrote to me on Christmas Eve) is in bed. Katie, who has been ill of low nervous fever, was brought here yesterday from London. She bore the journey much better than I expected, and so I hope will soon recover. This is my little stock of news.

I begin to discover in your riper years, that you have been secretly vain of your handwriting all your life. For I swear I see no change in it! What it always was since I first knew it (a year or two !) it *is*. This I will maintain against all comers.

Ever affectionately, my dearest Macready.

[ANONYMOUS]

OFFICE OF "ALL THE YEAR ROUND," Tuesday, Feb. 5th, 1867.

Dear Sir:

I have looked at the larger half of the first volume of your novel, and have pursued the more difficult points of the story through the other two volumes.

13

You will, of course, receive my opinion as that of an individual writer and student of art, who by no means claims to be infallible.

I think you are too ambitious, and that you have not sufficient knowledge of life or character to venture on so comprehensive an attempt. Evidences of inexperience in every way, and of your power being far below the situations that you imagine, present themselves to me in almost every page I have read. It would greatly surprise me if you found a publisher for this story, on trying your fortune in that line, or derived anything from it but weariness and bitterness of spirit.

On the evidence thus put before me, I cannot even entirely satisfy myself that you have the faculty of authorship latent within you. If you have not, and yet pursue a vocation towards which you have no call, you cannot choose but be a wretched man. Let me counsel you to have the patience to form yourself carefully, and the courage to renounce the endeavour if you cannot establish your case on a very much smaller scale. You see around you every day, how many outlets there are for short pieces of fiction in all kinds. Try if you can achieve any success within these modest limits (I have practised in my time what I preach to you), and in the meantime put your three volumes away.

Faithfully yours.

P.S.—Your MS. will be returned separately from this office.

[TO MR. F. D. FINLAY][1]

GAD'S HILL PLACE, HIGHAM BY ROCHESTER KENT,
Tuesday, Sept. 3d, 1867.

This is to certify that the undersigned victim of a periodical paragraph-disease, which usually breaks out once in every seven years (proceeding to England by the overland route to India and per Cunard line to America, where it strikes the base of the Rocky Mountains, and, rebounding to Europe, perishes on the steppes of Russia), is *not* in a "critical state of health," and has *not* consulted "eminent surgeons," and never was better in his life, and is *not* recommended to proceed to the United States for "cessation from literary labour," and has not had so much as a headache for twenty years.

CHARLES DICKENS.

[TO MR. JAMES T. FIELDS]

October, 1867.

My dear Fields :

. . . . . .

Reverting to the preposterous fabrication of the London correspondent, the statement that I ever

---

[1] Contradicting a newspaper report of his being in a critical state of health.

talked about "these fellows" who republished my books or pretended to know (what I don't know at this instant) who made how much out of them, or ever talked of their sending me "conscience money," is as grossly and completely false as the statement that I ever said anything to the effect that I could not be expected to have an interest in the American people. And nothing can by any possibility be falser than that. Again and again in these pages (*All the Year Round*) have I expressed my interest in them. You will see it in the *Child's History of England*. You will see it in the last preface to *American Notes*. Every American who has ever spoken with me in London, Paris, or where not, knows whether I have frankly said, "You could have no better introduction to me than your country." And for years and years when I have been asked about reading in America, my invariable reply has been, "I have so many friends there, and constantly receive so many earnest letters from personally unknown readers there, that, but for domestic reasons, I would go to-morrow." I think I must, in the confidential intercourse between you and me, have written you to this effect more than once.

   .   .   .   .   .   .

> Ever, my dear Fields,
>> Heartily and affectionately yours.

[TO MR. THORNBURY]

GAD'S HILL, Saturday, 5th October, 1867.

My dear Thornbury :

Behold the best of my judgment on your questions.[1]

Susan Hopley and Jonathan Bradford? No. Too well known.

London Strikes and Spitalfields Cutters? Yes.

Fighting FitzGerald? Never mind him.

Duel of Lord Mohun and Duke of Hamilton? Ye-e-es.

Irish Abductions? I think not.

Brunswick Theatre? More Yes than No.

Theatrical Farewells? Yes.

Bow Street Runners (as compared with Modern Detectives)? Yes.

Vauxhall and Ranelagh in the Last Century? Most decidedly. Don't forget Miss Burney.

Smugglers? No. Overdone.

Lacenaire? No. Ditto.

Madame Laffarge? No. Ditto.

Fashionable Life Last Century? Most decidedly yes.

Debates on the Slave Trade? Yes, generally. But beware of the Pirates, as we did them in the beginning of *Household Words.*

[1] As to subjects for articles in *All the Year Round.*

Certainly I acquit you of all blame in the Bedford case. But one cannot do otherwise than sympathise with a son who is reasonably tender of his father's memory. And no amount of private correspondence, we must remember, reaches the readers of a printed and published statement.

I told you some time ago that I believed the arsenic in Eliza Fenning's case to have been administered by the apprentice. I never was more convinced of anything in my life than of the girl's innocence, and I want words in which to express my indignation at the muddle-headed story of that parsonic blunderer whose audacity and conceit distorted some words that fell from her in the last days of her baiting.

Ever faithfully yours.

[TO MISS DICKENS]

PARKER HOUSE, BOSTON, Thursday, Nov. 21st, 1867.

I arrived here on Tuesday night, after a very slow passage from Halifax against head-winds. All the tickets for the first four readings here (all yet announced) were sold immediately on their being issued.

You know that I begin on the 2d of December with "Carol" and "Trial?" Shall be heartily glad to begin to count the readings off.

This is an immense hotel, with all manner of white marble public passages and public rooms. I live in a corner high up, and have a hot and cold bath in my bedroom (communicating with the sitting-room), and comforts not in existence when I was here before. The cost of living is enormous, but happily we can afford it. I dine to-day with Longfellow, Emerson, Holmes, and Agassiz. Longfellow was here yesterday. Perfectly white in hair and beard, but a remarkably handsome and notable-looking man. The city has increased enormously in five-and-twenty years. It has grown more mercantile—is like Leeds mixed with Preston, and flavoured with New Brighton; but for smoke and fog you substitute an exquisitely bright light air. I found my rooms beautifully decorated (by Mrs. Fields) with choice flowers, and set off by a number of good books. I am not much persecuted by people in general, as Dolby has happily made up his mind that the less I am exhibited for nothing the better. So our men sit outside the room door and wrestle with mankind.

We had speech-making and singing in the saloon of the Cuba after the last dinner of the voyage. I think I have acquired a higher reputation from drawing out the captain, and getting him to take the second in "All's Well," and likewise in "There's not in the wide world" (your parent tak-

ing first), than from anything previously known of
me on these shores. I hope the effect of these
achievements may not dim the lustre of the readings. We also sang (with a Chicago lady, and a
strong-minded woman from I don't know where)
"Auld Lang Syne," with a tender melancholy, ex-
pressive of having all four been united from our
cradles. The more dismal we were, the more delighted the company were. Once (when we pad-
dled i' the burn) the captain took a little cruise
round the compass on his own account, touching
at the "Canadian Boat Song," and taking in sup-
plies at "Jubilate," "Seas between us braid ha'
roared," and roared like the seas themselves. Finally, I proposed the ladies in a speech that con-
vulsed the stewards, and we closed with a brilliant
success. But when you dine with Mr. Forster, ask
him to read to you how we got on at church in a
heavy sea. Hillard has just been in and sent his
love "to those dear girls." He has grown much
older. He is now District Attorney of the State
of Massachusetts, which is a very good office. Best
love to your aunt and Katie, and Charley and all
his house, and all friends.

[TO MR. CHARLES DICKENS]

PARKER HOUSE, BOSTON, U. S., Saturday, Nov. 30th, 1867.

My dear Charley :

You will have heard before now how fortunate I
was on my voyage, and how I was not sick for a
moment. These screws are tremendous ships for
carrying on, and for rolling, and their vibration is
rather distressing. But my little cabin, being
for'ard of the machinery, was in the best part of
the vessel, and I had as much air in it, night and
day, as I chose. The saloon being kept absolutely
without air, I mostly dined in my own den, in spite
of my being allotted the post of honour on the
right hand of the captain.

. . . . . .

As they don't seem (Americans who have heard
me on their travels excepted) to have the least idea
here of what the readings are like, and as they are
accustomed to mere readings out of a book, I am
inclined to think the excitement will increase when
I shall have begun. Everybody is very kind and
considerate, and I have a number of old friends
here, at the Bar and connected with the University.
I am now negotiating to bring out the dramatic
version of *No Thoroughfare* at New York. It is
quite upon the cards that it may turn up trumps.

I was interrupted in that place by a call from my old secretary in the States, Mr. Putnam. It was quite affecting to see his delight in meeting his old master again. And when I told him that Anne was married, and that I had (unacknowledged) grand-children, he laughed and cried together. I suppose you don't remember Longfellow, though he remembers you in a black velvet frock very well. He is now white-haired and white-bearded, but remarkably handsome. He still lives in his old house, where his beautiful wife was burnt to death. I dined with him the other day, and could not get the terrific scene out of my imagination. She was in a blaze in an instant, rushed into his arms with a wild cry, and never spoke afterwards.

My love to Bessie, and to Mekitty, and all the babbies. I will lay this by until Tuesday morning, and then add a final line to it.

Ever, my dear Charley, your affectionate Father.

Tuesday, Dec. 3d, 1867.

Success last night beyond description or exagger-ation. The whole city is quite frantic about it to-day, and it is impossible that prospects could be more brilliant.

[TO MISS DICKENS]

PARKER HOUSE, BOSTON, Sunday, Dec. 1st, 1867.

. . . . . .

I have been going on very well. A horrible custom obtains in these parts of asking you to dinner
somewhere at half-past two, and to supper somewhere else about eight. I have run this gauntlet
more than once, and its effect is, that there is no
day for any useful purpose, and that the length of
the evening is multiplied by a hundred. Yesterday
I dined with a club at half-past two, and came
back here at half-past eight, with a general impression that it was at least two o'clock in the morning.
Two days before I dined with Longfellow at half-
past two, and came back at eight, supposing it to
be midnight. To-day we have a state dinner-party
in our rooms at six, Mr. and Mrs. Fields, and Mr.
and Mrs. Bigelow. (He is a friend of Forster's,
and was American Minister in Paris.) There are
no negro waiters here, all the servants are Irish—
willing, but not able. The dinners and wines are
very good. I keep our own rooms well ventilated
by opening the windows, but no window is ever
opened in the halls or passages, and they are so
overheated by a great furnace, that they make me
faint and sick. The air is like that of a pre-Adam-
ite ironing-day in full blast. Your respected parent

is immensely popular in Boston society, and its
cordiality and unaffected heartiness are charming.
I wish I could carry it with me.

The leading New York papers have sent men over
for to-morrow night with instructions to telegraph
columns of descriptions. Great excitement and expectation everywhere. Fields says he has looked
forward to it so long that he knows he will die at
five minutes to eight.

At the New York barriers, where the tickets are
on sale and the people ranged as at the Paris theatres, speculators went up and down offering "twenty
dollars for anybody's place." The money was in no
case accepted. One man sold two tickets for the
second, third, and fourth night for "one ticket for
the first, fifty dollars" (about seven pounds ten
shillings), "and a brandy cocktail," which is an iced
bitter drink. The weather has been rather muggy
and languid until yesterday, when there was the
coldest wind blowing that I ever felt. In the night
it froze very hard, and to-day the sky is beautiful.

Tuesday, Dec. 3d.

Most magnificent reception last night, and most
signal and complete success. Nothing could be
more triumphant. The people will hear of nothing
else and talk of nothing else. Nothing that was

ever done here, they all agree, evoked any approach to such enthusiasm. I was quite as cool and quick as if I were reading at Greenwich, and went at it accordingly.

.   .   .   .   .   .

[TO MISS DICKENS]

WESTMINSTER HOTEL, IRVING PLACE, NEW YORK CITY,
Wednesday, Dec. 11th, 1867.

Amazing success here.   A very fine audience ; *far better than that at Boston.*   Great reception.   Great, "Carol" and "Trial," on the first night ; still greater, "Copperfield" and "Bob," on the second. Dolby sends you a few papers by this post.   You will see from their tone what a success it is.

I cannot pay this letter, because I give it at the latest moment to the mail-officer, who is going on board the Cunard packet in charge of the mails, and who is staying in this house.   We are now selling (at the hall) the tickets for the four readings of next week.   At nine o'clock this morning there were two thousand people in waiting, and they had begun to assemble in the bitter cold as early as two o'clock.   All night long Dolby and our man have been stamping tickets.   (Immediately over my head, by-the-bye, and keeping me awake.)   This hotel is quite as quiet as Mivart's, in Brook Street.   It is not very much larger.   There are American hotels close by, with five hundred bed-rooms, and I don't know how many boarders; but this is conducted on what is called "the European principle," and is an admirable mixture of a first-class French and English house. I keep a very smart carriage and pair; and if you were to behold me driving out, furred up to the moustache, with furs on the coach-boy and on the driver, and with an immense white, red, and yellow striped rug for a covering, you would suppose me to be of Hungarian or Polish nationality.

Will you report the success here to Mr. Forster with my love, and tell him he shall hear from me by next mail?

Dolby sends his kindest regards. He is just come in from our ticket sales, and has put such an immense untidy heap of paper money on the table that it looks like a family wash. He hardly ever dines, and is always tearing about at unreasonable hours. He works very hard.

My best love to your aunt (to whom I will write next), and to Katie, and to both the Charleys, and all the Christmas circle, not forgetting Chorley, to whom give my special remembrance. You may get this by Christmas Day. *We* shall have to keep it travelling from Boston here; for I read at Boston on the 23d and 24th, and here again on the 26th.

[TO MISS HOGARTH]

Boston, Sunday, Dec. 22d, 1867.

Coming here from New York last night (after a detestable journey), I was delighted to find your letter of the 6th. I read it at my ten o'clock dinner with the greatest interest and pleasure, and then we talked of home till we went to bed.

Our tour is now being made out, and I hope to be able to send it in my next letter home, which will be to Mamie, from whom I have *not* heard (as you thought I had) by the mail that brought out yours. After very careful consideration I have reversed Dolby's original plan, and have decided on taking Baltimore, Washington, Cincinnati, *Chicago* (!), St. Louis, and a few other places nearer here, instead of staying in New York. My reason is that we are doing immensely, both at New York and here, and that I am sure it is in the peculiar character of the people to prize a thing the more the less easily attainable it is made. Therefore, I want, by absence, to get the greatest rush and pressure upon the five farewell readings in New York in April. All our announced readings are already crammed.

When we got here last Saturday night, we found that Mrs. Fields had not only garnished the rooms

with flowers, but also with holly (with real red berries) and festoons of moss dependent from the look-
ing-glasses and picture frames. She is one of the
dearest little women in the world. The homely
Christmas look of the place quite affected us. Yesterday we dined at her house, and there was a plum-
pudding brought on blazing, and not to be sur-
passed in any house in England. There is a certain
Captain Dolliver, belonging to the Boston Custom
House, who came off in the little steamer that
brought me ashore from the Cuba. He took it into
his head that he would have a piece of English mis-
tletoe brought out in this week's Cunard, which
should be laid upon my breakfast-table. And there
it was this morning. In such affectionate touches
as this, these New England people are especially
amiable.

As a general rule, you may lay it down that whatever you see about me in the papers is not true.
But although my voyage out was of that highly hi-
larious description that you first made known to
me, you may *generally* lend a more believing ear to
the Philadelphia correspondent of *The Times*. I
don't know him, but I know the source from which
he derives his information, and it is a very respectable one.

Did I tell you in a former letter from here, to
tell Anne, with her old master's love, that I had

seen Putnam, my old secretary? Gray, and with several front teeth out, but I would have known him anywhere. He is coming to "Copperfield" tonight, accompanied by his wife and daughter, and is in the seventh heaven at having his tickets given him.

Our hotel in New York was on fire *again* the other night. But fires in this country are quite matters of course. There was a large one there at four this morning, and I don't think a single night has passed since I have been under the protection of the Eagle, but I have heard the fire bells dolefully clanging all over the city.

Dolby sends his kindest regard. His hair has become quite white, the effect, I suppose, of the climate. He is so universally hauled over the coals (for no reason on earth), that I fully expect to hear him, one of these nights, assailed with a howl when he precedes me to the platform steps. You may conceive what the low newspapers are here, when one of them yesterday morning had, as an item of news, the intelligence: "Dickens's Readings. The chap calling himself Dolby got drunk last night, and was locked up in a police-station for fighting an Irishman." I don't find that anybody is shocked by this liveliness.

My love to all, and to Mrs. Hulkes and the boy. By-the-bye, when we left New York for this place,

14

Dolby called my amazed attention to the circumstance that Scott was leaning his head against the side of the carriage and weeping bitterly. I asked him what was the matter, and he replied : " The owdacious treatment of the luggage, which was more outrageous than a man could bear." I told him not to make a fool of himself ; but they do knock it about cruelly. I think every trunk we have is already broken.

I must leave off, as I am going out for a walk in a bright sunlight and a complete break-up of· the frost and snow. I am much better than I have been during the last week, but have a cold.

[TO MISS DICKENS]

WESTMINSTER HOTEL, IRVING PLACE, NEW YORK CITY,
Thursday, Dec. 26th, 1867.

I got your aunt's last letter at Boston yesterday, Christmas Day morning, when I was starting at eleven o'clock to come back to this place. I wanted it very much, for I had a frightful cold (English colds are nothing to those of this country), and was exceedingly depressed and miserable. Not that I had any reason but illness for being so, since the Bostonians had been quite astounding in their demonstrations. I never saw anything like them on Christmas Eve. But it is a bad country to be unwell and travelling in ; you are one of say a hundred people in a heated car, with a great stove in it, and all the little windows closed, and the hurrying and banging about are indescribable. The atmosphere is detestable, and the motion often all but intolerable. However, we got our dinner here at eight o'clock, and plucked up a little, and I made some hot gin punch to drink a merry Christmas to all at home in. But it must be confessed that we were both very dull.

. . . . . .

If I do not send a letter to Katie by this mail, it will be because I shall probably be obliged to go across the water to Brooklyn to-morrow to see a church, in which it is proposed that I shall read ! ! ! Horrible visions of being put in the pulpit already beset me. And whether the audience will be in pews is another consideration which greatly disturbs my mind. No paper ever comes out without a leader on Dolby, who of course reads them all, and never can understand why I don't, in which he is called all the bad names in (and not in) the language.

We always call him P. H. Dolby now, in consequence of one of these graceful specimens of literature describing him as the " pudding-headed."

I fear that when we travel he will have to be always before me, so that I may not see him six times

in as many weeks.   However, I shall have done a
fourth of the whole this very next week !

Best love to your aunt, and the boys, and Katie,
and Charley, and all true friends.

Friday.

I managed to read last night, but it was as much
as I could do.   To-day I am so very unwell, that I
have sent for a doctor ; he has just been, and is in
doubt whether I shall not have to stop reading for
a while.

[TO MISS DICKENS]

WESTMINSTER HOTEL, IRVING PLACE, NEW YORK,
Monday, Dec. 30th, 1867.

I am getting all right again.   I have not been
well, been very low, and have been obliged to have
a doctor ; a very agreeable fellow indeed, who soon
turned out to be an old friend of Olliffe's.[1]   He
has set me on my legs and taken his leave "pro-
fessionally," though he means to give me a call
now and then.

.   .   .   .   .   .

Nothing is being played here scarcely that is
not founded on my books—*Cricket, Oliver Twist,
Our Mutual Friend*, and I don't know what else,
every night.   I can't get down Broadway for my

<hr>

[1] Dr. Fordyce Barker.

own portrait; and yet I live almost as quietly in this hotel, as if I were at the office, and go in and out by a side door just as I might there.

I go back to Boston on Saturday to read there on Monday and Tuesday. Then I am back here, and keep within six or seven hours' journey of here-abouts till February. My further movements shall be duly reported as the details are arranged.

I shall be curious to know who were at Gad's Hill on Christmas Day, and how you (as they say in this country) "got along." It is exceedingly cold here again, after two or three quite spring days.

[TO MISS HOGARTH]

WESTMINSTER HOTEL, IRVING PLACE, NEW YORK,
Friday, Jan. 3rd, 1868.

My dearest Georgy :

I received yours of the 19th from Gad's and the office this morning. I read here to-night, and go back to Boston to-morrow, to read there Monday and Tuesday.

To-night I read out the first quarter of my list. Our houses have been very fine here, but have never quite recovered the Dolby uproar. It seems impossible to devise any scheme for getting the tickets into the people's hands without the intervention of speculators. The people *will not* help themselves ;

and, of course, the speculators and all other such prowlers throw as great obstacles in Dolby's way (an Englishman's) as they possibly can. He may be a little injudicious into the bargain. Last night, for instance, he met one of the " ushers " (who show people to their seats) coming in with Kelly. It is against orders that anyone employed in front should go out during the readings, and he took this man to task in the British manner. Instantly the free and independent usher put on his hat and walked off. Seeing which, all the other free and independent ushers (some twenty in number) put on *their* hats and walked off, leaving us absolutely devoid and destitute of a staff for to-night. One has since been improvised ; but it was a small matter to raise a stir and ill will about, especially as one of our men was equally in fault.

.   .   .   .   .   .

Tell Plorn, with my love, that I think he will find himself much interested at that college,[1] and that it is very likely he may make some acquaintances there that will thereafter be pleasant and useful to him. Sir Sidney Dacres is the best of friends. I have a letter from Mrs. Hulkes by this post, wherein the boy encloses a violet, now lying on the table before me. Let her know that it arrived safely, and retaining its colour. I took it for granted that Mary

[1] The Agricultural College, Cirencester.

would have asked Chorley for Christmas Day, and
am very glad she ultimately did so. I am sorry
that Harry lost his prize, but believe it was not his
fault. Let *him* know *that*, with my love. I would
have written to him by this mail in answer to his,
but for other occupation. Did I tell you that my
landlord made me a drink (brandy, rum, and snow
the principal ingredients) called a "Rocky Mountain sneezer"? Or that the favourite drink before
you get up is an "eye-opener"? Or that Roberts
(second landlord), no sooner saw me on the night of
the first fire, than, with his property blazing, he insisted on taking me down into a roomful of hot
smoke to drink brandy and water with him? We
have not been on fire again, by-the-bye, more than
once.

[TO MISS HOGARTH]

PARKER HOUSE, BOSTON, U. S., Jan. 4th, 1868.

I write to you by this opportunity, though I
really have nothing to tell you. The work is hard
and the climate is hard. We made a tremendous hit
last night with "Nickleby" and "Boots," which the
Bostonians certainly on the whole appreciate more
than "Copperfield!" Dolby is always going about
with an immense bundle that looks like a sofa
cushion, but it is in reality paper money; and always works like a Trojan. His business at night is

a mere nothing, for these people are so accustomed
to take care of themselves, that one of these immense audiences will fall into their places with an
ease amazing to a frequenter of St. James's Hall.
And the certainty with which they are all in, before
I go on, is a very acceptable mark of respect. I
must add, too, that although there is a conventional
familiarity in the use of one's name in the newspapers as "Dickens," "Charlie," and what not, I do
not in the least see that familiarity in the writers
themselves. An inscrutable tone obtains in journal-
ism, which a stranger cannot understand. If I say
in common courtesy to one of them, when Dolby
introduces, "I am much obliged to you for your interest in me," or so forth, he seems quite shocked,
and has a bearing of perfect modesty and propriety.
I am rather inclined to think that they suppose
their printed tone to be the public's love of smartness, but it is immensely difficult to make out. All
I can as yet make out is, that my perfect freedom
from bondage, and at any moment to go on or leave
off, or otherwise do as I like, is the only safe position to occupy.

Again ; there are two apparently irreconcilable
contrasts here. Down below in this hotel every
night are the bar loungers, dram drinkers, drunk-
ards, swaggerers, loafers, that one might find in a
Boucicault play. Within half an hour is Cam-

bridge, where a delightful domestic life—simple, self-respectful, cordial, and affectionate—is seen in an admirable aspect. All New England is primitive and puritanical. All about and around it is a puddle of mixed human mud, with no such quality in it. Perhaps I may in time sift out some tolerably intelligible whole, but I certainly have not done so yet. It is a good sign, may be, that it all seems immensely more difficult to understand than it was when I was here before.

Felton left two daughters. I have only seen the eldest, a very sensible, frank, pleasant girl of eight-and-twenty, perhaps, rather like him in the face. A striking-looking daughter of Hawthorne's (who is also dead) came into my room last night. The day has slipped on to three o'clock, and I must get up "Domber" for to-night. Hence this sudden break off. Best love to Mamie, and to Katie and Charley Collins.

[TO MR. W. WILKIE COLLINS]

WESTMINSTER HOTEL, NEW YORK, Sunday, Jan. 12th, 1868.

My dear Wilkie :

.   .   .   .   .   .

Being at Boston last Sunday, I took it into my head to go over the medical school, and survey the holes and corners in which that extraordinary murder was done by Webster. There was the

furnace—stinking horribly, as if the dismembered
pieces were still inside it—and there are all the
grim spouts, and sinks, and chemical appliances,
and what not. At dinner, afterwards, Longfellow
told me a terrific story. He dined with Webster
within a year of the murder, one of a party of ten
or twelve. As they sat at their wine, Webster suddenly ordered the lights to be turned out, and a
bowl of some burning mineral to be placed on the
table, that the guests might see how ghostly it
made them look. As each man stared at all the
rest in the weird light, all were horrified to see
Webster *with a rope round his neck*, holding it up,
over the bowl, with his head jerked on one side,
and his tongue lolled out, representing a man being
hanged!

Poking into his life and character, I find (what I
would have staked my head upon) that he was always a cruel man.

So no more at present from,

My dear Wilkie, yours ever affectionately.

[TO MISS HOGARTH]

WESTMINSTER HOTEL, NEW YORK, Sunday, Jan. 12th, 1868.

As I am off to Philadelphia this evening, I may
as well post my letter here. I have scarcely a word
of news.

.   .   .   .   .   .

On Wednesday I come back here for my four
church readings at Brooklyn. Each evening an
enormous ferry-boat will convey me and my state
carriage (not to mention half-a-dozen waggons, and
any number of people, and a few score of horses)
across the river, and will bring me back again. The
sale of tickets there was an amazing scene. The
noble army of speculators are now furnished (this is
literally true, and I am quite serious), each man with
a straw mattress, a little bag of bread and meat, two
blankets, and a bottle of whiskey. With this outfit
they lie down in line on the pavement the whole night
before the tickets are sold, generally taking up
their position at about ten. It being severely cold
at Brooklyn, they made an immense bonfire in the
street—a narrow street of wooden houses!—which
the police turned out to extinguish. A general
fight then took place, out of which the people farth-
est off in the line rushed bleeding when they saw a
chance of displacing others near the door, and put
their mattresses in those places, and then held on
by the iron rails. At eight in the morning Dolby
appeared with the tickets in a portmanteau. He
was immediately saluted with a roar of "Halloa
Dolby! So Charley has let you have the carriage,
has he, Dolby! How is he, Dolby! Don't drop
the tickets, Dolby! Look alive, Dolby!" etc. etc.
etc., in the midst of which he proceeded to busi-

ness, and concluded (as usual) by giving universal dissatisfaction.

He is now going off upon a little journey "to look over the ground and cut back again." This little journey (to Chicago) is fifteen hundred miles on end, by railway, and back again!

  .   .   .   .   .   .

Did I tell you that the severity of the weather, and the heat of the intolerable furnaces, dry the hair and break the nails of strangers? There is not a complete nail in the whole British suite, and my hair cracks again when I brush it. (I am losing my hair with great rapidity, and what I don't lose is getting very grey.)

The Cuba will bring this. She has a jolly new captain—Moody, of the Java—and her people rushed into the reading, the other night, captain-headed, as if I were their peculiar property. Please God I shall come home in her, in my old cabin ; leaving here on the 22nd of April, and finishing my eighty-fourth reading on the previous night! It is likely enough that I shall read and go straight on board.

I think this is all my poor stock of intelligence. By-the-bye, on the last Sunday in the old year, I lost my old year's pocket-book, "which," as Mr. Pepys would add, "do trouble me mightily." Give me Katie's new address ; I haven't got it.

[TO MISS DICKENS]

PHILADELPHIA, Monday, Jan. 13th, 1868.

I write you this note, a day later than your aunt's, not because I have anything to add to the little I have told her, but because you may like to have it. We arrived here last night toward twelve o'clock, more than an hour after our time. This is one of the immense American hotels (it is called the Continental) ; but I find myself just as quiet here as elsewhere. Everything is very good indeed, the waiter is German, and the greater part of the house servants seem to be coloured people. The town is very clean, and the day as blue and bright as a fine Italian day. But it freezes very hard. All the tickets being sold here for six nights (three visits of two nights each), the suite complain of want of excitement already, having been here ten hours ! Mr. and Mrs. Barney Williams, with a couple of servants, and a pretty little child-daughter, were in the train each night, and I talked with them a good deal. They are reported to have made an enormous fortune by acting among the Californian gold-diggers. My cold is no better, for the cars are so intolerably hot, that I was often obliged to go and stand upon the break outside, and then the frosty air was biting indeed. The great man of this place is one Mr.

Childs, a newspaper proprietor, and he is so exactly like Mr. Esse in all conceivable respects except being an inch or so taller, that I was quite confounded when I saw him waiting for me at the station (always called depôt here) with his carriage. During the last two or three days, Dolby and I have been making up accounts, which are excellently kept by Mr. Osgood, and I find them amazing, quite, in their results.

[TO MR. SAMUEL CARTWRIGHT]

BALTIMORE, WEDNESDAY, Jan. 29th, 1868.

My dear Cartwright :

As I promised to report myself to you from this side of the Atlantic, and as I have some leisure this morning, I am going to lighten my conscience by keeping my word.

I am going on at a great pace and with immense success. Next week, at Washington, I shall, please God, have got through half my readings. The remaining half are all arranged, and they will carry me into the third week of April. It is very hard work, but it is brilliantly paid. The changes that I find in the country generally (this place is the least changed of any I have yet seen) exceed my utmost expectations. I had been in New York a couple of days before I began to recognise it at all ;

and the handsomest part of Boston was a black swamp when I saw it five-and-twenty years ago. Considerable advances, too, have been made socially. Strange to say, the railways and railway arrangements (both exceedingly defective) seem to have stood still while all other things have been moving.

One of the most comical spectacles I have ever seen in my life was " church," with a heavy sea on, in the saloon of the Cunard steamer coming out. The officiating minister, an extremely modest young man, was brought in between two big stewards, exactly as if he were coming up to the scratch in a prize-fight. The ship was rolling and pitching so, that the two big stewards had to stop and watch their opportunity of making a dart at the reading-desk with their reverend charge, during which pause he held on, now by one steward and now by the other, with the feeblest expression of countenance and no legs whatever. At length they made a dart at the wrong moment, and one steward was immediately beheld alone in the extreme perspective, while the other and the reverend gentleman *held on by the mast* in the middle of the saloon—which the latter embraced with both arms, as if it were his wife. All this time the congregation was breaking up into sects and sliding away ; every sect (as in nature) pounding the other sect. And when

at last the reverend gentleman had been tumbled
into his place, the desk (a loose one, put upon the
dining-table) deserted from the church bodily, and
went over to the purser. The scene was so extraordinarily ridiculous, and was made so much more so
by the exemplary gravity of all concerned in it, that
I was obliged to leave before the service began.

This is one of the places where Butler carried it
with so high a hand in the war, and where the ladies used to spit when they passed a Northern soldier. It still wears, I fancy, a look of sullen remembrance. (The ladies are remarkably handsome,
with an Eastern look upon them, dress with a strong
sense of colour, and make a brilliant audience.)
The ghost of slavery haunts the houses ; and the
old, untidy, incapable, lounging, shambling black
serves you as a free man. Free of course he ought
to be ; but the stupendous absurdity of making him
a voter glares out of every roll of his eye, stretch of
his mouth, and bump of his head. I have a strong
impression that the race must fade out of the States
very fast. It never can hold its own against a striv-
ing, restless, shifty people. In the penitentiary
here, the other day, in a room full of all blacks (too
dull to be taught any of the work in hand), was one
young brooding fellow, very like a black rhinoceros.
He sat glowering at life, as if it were just endurable
at dinner time, until four of his fellows began to

sing, most unmelodiously, a part song. He then set up a dismal howl, and pounded his face on a form. I took him to have been rendered quite desperate by having learnt anything. I send my kind regard to Mrs. Cartwright, and sincerely hope that she and you have no new family distresses or anxieties. My standing address is the Westminster Hotel, Irving Place, New York City. And I am always, my dear Cartwright,

Cordially yours.

[TO MISS DICKENS]

WASHINGTON, Tuesday, Feb. 4th, 1868.

I began here last night with great success. The hall being small, the prices were raised to three dollars each ticket. The audience was a superior one, composed of the foremost public men and their families. At the end of the "Carol" they gave a great break out, and applauded, I really believe, for five minutes. You would suppose them to be Manchester shillings instead of Washington half sovereigns. Immense enthusiasm.

. . . . . .

I dined (against my rules) with Charles Sumner on Sunday, he having been an old friend of mine. Mr. Secretary Stanton (War Minister) was there. He is a man of a very remarkable memory, and

15

famous for his acquaintance with the minutest details of my books. Give him any passage anywhere,
and he will instantly cap it and go on with the
context. He was commander-in-chief of all the
Northern forces concentrated here, and never went
to sleep at night without first reading something
from my books, which were always with him. I put
him through a pretty severe examination, but he
was better up than I was.

The gas was very defective indeed last night, and
I began with a small speech, to the effect that I
must trust to the brightness of their faces for the
illumination of mine ; this was taken greatly. In
the "Carol," a most ridiculous incident occurred all
of a sudden. I saw a dog look out from among the
seats into the centre aisle, and look very intently
at me. The general attention being fixed on me,
I don't think anybody saw the dog ; but I felt
so sure of his turning up again and barking,
that I kept my eye wandering about in search of
him. He was a very comic dog, and it was well for
me that I was reading a very comic part of the book.
But when he bounced out into the centre aisle
again, in an entirely new place (still looking intently
at me) and tried the effect of a bark upon my proceedings, I was seized with such a paroxysm of
laughter, that it communicated itself to the audience,
and we roared at one another loud and long. The

President has sent to me twice, and I am going to see him to-morrow. He has a whole row for his family every night.

.   .   .   .   .   .

[TO MR. CHARLES LANMAN]

WASHINGTON, February 5th, 1868.

My dear Sir :

.   .   .   .   .   .

Your reference to my dear friend Washington Irving renews the vivid impressions reawakened in my mind at Baltimore the other day. I saw his fine face for the last time in that city. He came there from New York to pass a day or two with me before I went westward, and they were made among the most memorable of my life by his delightful fancy and genial humour. Some unknown admirer of his books and mine sent to the hotel a most enormous mint julep, wreathed with flowers. We sat, one on either side of it, with great solemnity (it filled a respectable-sized paper), but the solemnity was of very short duration. It was quite an enchanted julep, and carried us among innumerable people and places that we both knew. The julep held out far into the night, and my memory never saw him afterward otherwise than as bending over it, with his straw, with an attempted gravity (after some anecdote, involving some wonderfully droll

and delicate observation of character), and then, as
his eyes caught mine, melting into that captivating
laugh of his which was the brightest and best I have
ever heard.

Dear Sir, with many thanks, faithfully yours.

[TO MISS DICKENS]

BALTIMORE, U. S., Tuesday, Feb. 11th, 1868.

The weather has been desperately severe, and my
cold quite as bad as ever.   I couldn't help laughing
at myself on my birthday at Washington.   It was
observed as much as though I were a little boy.
Flowers and garlands (of the most exquisite kind)
bloomed all over the room ; letters radiant with
good wishes poured in ; a shirt pin, a handsome sil-
ver travelling bottle, a set of gold shirt studs, and
a set of gold sleeve links were on the dinner-table.
After "Boots," at night, the whole audience rose and
remained (Secretaries of State, President's family,
Judges of Supreme Court, and so forth) standing
and cheering until I went back to the table and
made them a little speech.   On the same august day
of the year I was received by the President, a man
with a very remarkable and determined face.   Each
of us looked at each other very hard, and each of us
managed the interview (I think) to the satisfaction
of the other.   In the outer room was sitting a cer-

tain sunburnt General Blair, with many evidences of the war upon him. He got up to shake hands with me, and then I found he had been out in the prairie with me, five-and-twenty years ago. That afternoon my "catarrh" was in such a state that Charles Sumner, coming in at five o'clock and finding me covered with mustard poultice, and apparently voiceless, turned to Dolby and said : "Surely, Mr. Dolby, it is impossible that he can read to-night." Says Dolby : "Sir, I have told the dear Chief so four times to-day, and I have been very anxious. But you have no idea how he will change when he gets to the little table." After five minutes of the little table, I was not (for the time) even hoarse. The frequent experience of this return of force when it is wanted saves me a vast amount of anxiety.

.   .   .   .   .   .

[TO MR. HENRY FIELDING DICKENS]

BALTIMORE, U. S., Tuesday, Feb. 11th, 1868.

My dear Harry :
   I should have written to you before now, but for constant and arduous occupation.

.   .   .   .   .   .

I am very glad to hear of the success of your reading, and still more glad that you went at it in down-

right earnest. I should never have made my success in life if I had been shy of taking pains, or if I
had not bestowed upon the least thing I have ever
undertaken exactly the same attention and care that
I have bestowed upon the greatest. Do everything
at your best. It was but this last year that I set
to and learned every word of my readings ; and
from ten years ago to last night, I have never read
to an audience but I have watched for an opportunity of striking out something better somewhere.
Look at such of my manuscripts as are in the
library at Gad's, and think of the patient hours
devoted year after year to single lines.

.   .   .   .   .   .

Ever, my dear Harry, your affectionate Father.

[TO M. CHARLES FECHTER]

WASHINGTON, February 24th, 1868.
My dear Fechter :

.   .   .   .   .   .

I am doing enormous business. It is a wearying
life, away from all I love, but I hope that the time
will soon begin to spin away. Among the many
changes that I find here is the comfortable change
that the people are in general extremely considerate, and very observant of my privacy. Even in this
place, I am really almost as much my own master as

if I were in an English country town. Generally, they are very good audiences indeed. They do not (I think) perceive touches of art to *be* art ; but they are responsive to the broad results of such touches. "Doctor Marigold" is a great favourite, and they laugh so unrestrainedly at "The Trial" from *Pickwick* (which you never heard), that it has grown about half as long again as it used to be.

If I could send you a " brandy cock-tail " by post I would. It is a highly meritorious dram, which I hope to present to you at Gad's. My New York landlord made me a "Rocky Mountain sneezer," which appeared to me to be compounded of all the spirits ever heard of in the world, with bitters, lemons, sugar, and snow. You can only make a true "sneezer" when the snow is lying on the ground.

There, my dear boy, my paper is out, and I am going to read "Copperfield." Count always on my fidelity and true attachment, and look out, as I have already said, for a distinguished visitor about Monday, the 4th of May.

Ever, my dear Fechter,

Your cordial and affectionate Friend.

[TO M. CHARLES FECHTER]

SYRACUSE, U. S. OF AMERICA,
Sunday Night, March 8th, 1868.

My dear Fechter :

I am here in a most wonderful out-of-the-world place, which looks as if it had begun to be built yesterday, and were going to be imperfectly knocked together with a nail or two the day after to-morrow. I am in the worst inn that ever was seen, and outside is a thaw that places the whole country under water. I have looked out of window for the people, and I can't find any people. I have tried all the wines in the house, and there are only two wines, for which you pay six shillings a bottle, or fifteen, according as you feel disposed to change the name of the thing you ask for. (The article never changes.) The bill of fare is " in French," and the principal article (the carte is printed) is "Paettie de shay." I asked the Irish waiter what this dish was, and he said : "It was the name the steward giv' to oyster patties—the Frinch name." These are the drinks you are to wash it down with: "Mooseux," "Abasinthe," "Curacco," "Marschine," "Annise," and "Margeaux!"

    •   •   •   •   •   •

I have had an American cold (the worst in the world) since Christmas Day. I read four times a week, with the most tremendous energy I can bring to bear upon it. I travel about pretty heavily. I am very resolute about calling on people, or receiving people, or dining out, and so save myself a great deal. I read in all sorts of places—churches, theatres, concert rooms, lecture halls. Every night I read I am described (mostly by people who have not the faintest notion of observing) from the sole of my boot to where the topmost hair of my head ought to be, but is not. Sometimes I am described as¹ being "evidently nervous;" sometimes it is rather taken ill that "Mr. Dickens is so extraordinarily composed." My eyes are blue, red, grey, white, green, brown, black, hazel, violet, and rainbow-coloured. I am like "a well-to-do American gentleman," and the Emperor of the French, with an occasional touch of the Emperor of China, and a deterioration from the attributes of our famous townsman, Rufus W. B. D. Dodge Grumsher Pickville. I say all sorts of things that I never said, go to all sorts of places that I never saw or heard of, and have done all manner of things (in some previous state of existence I suppose) that have quite escaped my memory. You ask your friend to describe what he is about. This is what he is about, every day and hour of his American life.

I hope to be back with you before you write to
me !

Ever, my dear Fechter,
        Your most affectionate and hearty Friend.

P.S.—Don't let Madame Fechter, or Marie, or
Paul forget me !

[TO MISS HOGARTH]

SYRACUSE, Sunday, March 8th, 1868.

As we shall probably be busy all day to-morrow,
I write this to-day, though it will not leave New
York until Wednesday. This is a very grim place
in a heavy thaw, and a most depressing one. The
hotel also is surprisingly bad, quite a triumph in
that way. We stood out for an hour in the melting
snow, and came in again, having to change completely. Then we sat down by the stove (no fire-
place), and there we are now. We were so afraid
to go to bed last night, the rooms were so close and
sour, that we played whist, double dummy, till we
couldn't bear each other any longer. We had an
old buffalo for supper, and an old pig for breakfast,
and we are going to have I don't know what for
dinner at six. In the public rooms downstairs, a
number of men (speechless) are sitting in rocking-

chairs, with their feet against the window-frames, staring out at window and spitting dolefully at intervals. Scott is in tears, and George the gasman is suborning people to go and clean the hall, which is a marvel of dirt. And yet we have taken considerably over three hundred pounds for to-morrow night!

[TO MR. W. C. MACREADY]

SPRINGFIELD, MASS., Saturday, March 21st, 1868.

My dearest Macready :

.   .   .   .   .   .

You would find the general aspect of America and Americans decidedly much improved. You would find immeasurably greater consideration and respect for your privacy than of old. You would find a steady change for the better everywhere, except (oddly enough) in the railroads generally, which seem to have stood still, while everything else has moved. But there is an exception westward. There the express trains have now a very delightful carriage called a "drawing-room car," literally a series of little private drawing-rooms, with sofas and a table in each, opening out of a little corridor. In each, too, is a large plate-glass window, with which you can do as you like. As you pay extra for this luxury, it may be regarded as the first move towards two classes of passengers. When the railroad straight away to San Francisco (in six days) shall be opened through, it will not only have these drawing-rooms, but sleeping-rooms too ; a bell in every little apartment communicating with a steward's pantry, a restaurant, a staff of servants, marble washing-stands, and a barber's shop! I looked into one of these cars a day or two ago, and it was very ingeniously arranged and quite complete.

.   .   .   .   .   .

I have seen all our Boston friends, except Curtis. Ticknor is dead. The rest are very little changed, except that Longfellow has a perfectly white flowing beard and long white hair. But he does not otherwise look old, and is infinitely handsomer than he was. I have been constantly with them all, and they have always talked much of you. It is the established joke that Boston is my "native place," and we hold all sorts of hearty foregatherings. They all come to every reading, and are always in a most delightful state of enthusiasm. They give me a parting dinner at the club, on the Thursday before Good Friday. To pass from Boston personal to New York theatrical, I will mention here that one of the proprietors of my New York hotel is one of the proprietors of Niblo's, and the most active. Consequently I have seen the *Black Crook* and the *White Fawn*, in majesty, from an arm-chair in the first entrance, P.S., more than once. Of these astonishing dramas, I beg to report (seriously) that I have found no human creature "behind" who has the slighest idea what they are about (upon my honour, my dearest Macready!), and that having some amiable small talk with a neat little Spanish woman, who is the *première danseuse*, I asked her, in joke, to let me measure her skirt with my dress glove. Holding the glove by the tip of the forefinger, I found the skirt to be just three gloves long, and yet its length was much in excess of the skirts of two hundred other ladies, whom the carpenters were at that moment getting into their places for a transformation scene, on revolving columns, on wires and "travellers" in iron cradles, up in the flies, down in the cellars, on every description of float that Wilmot, gone distracted, could imagine!

.   .   .   .   .   .

Niagara is not at all spoiled by a very dizzy-looking suspension bridge. Is to have another still nearer to the Horse-shoe opened in July. My last sight of that scene (last Sunday) was thus: We went up to the rapids above the Horse-shoe—say two miles from it—and through the great cloud of spray. Everything in the magnificent valley— buildings, forest, high banks, air, water, everything —was *made of rainbow*. Turner's most imaginative drawing in his finest day has nothing in it so ethereal, so gorgeous in fancy, so celestial. We said to one another (Dolby and I), "Let it for ever-more remain so," and shut our eyes and came away.

God bless you and all dear to you, my dear old Friend!

I am ever your affectionate and loving.

[TO MR. HENRY FIELDING DICKENS]

ADELPHI HOTEL, LIVERPOOL, Thursday, Oct. 15th, 1868.

My dear Harry :

I have your letter here this morning. I enclose you another cheque for twenty-five pounds, and I write to London by this post, ordering three dozen sherry, two dozen port, and three dozen light claret, to be sent down to you.

Now, observe attentively. We must have no shadow of debt. Square up everything whatsoever that it has been necessary to buy. Let not a farth-ing be outstanding on any account, when we begin together with your allowance. Be particular in the minutest detail.

I wish to have no secret from you in the relations we are to establish together, and I therefore send you Joe Chitty's letter bodily. Reading it, you will know exactly what I know, and will under-

stand that I treat you with perfect confidence. It
appears to me that an allowance of two hundred
and fifty pounds a year will be handsome for all
your wants, if I send you your wines. I mean this
to include your tailor's bills as well as every other
expense; and I strongly recommend you to buy
nothing in Cambridge, and to take credit for nothing but the clothes with which your tailor provides
you. As soon as you have got your furniture accounts in, let us wipe all those preliminary expenses
clean out, and I will then send you your first
quarter. We will count in it October, November,
and December; and your second quarter will begin
with the New Year. If you dislike, at first, taking
charge of so large a sum as sixty-two pounds ten
shillings, you can have your money from me half-
quarterly.

You know how hard I work for what I get, and I
think you know that I never had money help from
any human creature after I was a child. You know
that you are one of many heavy charges on me, and
that I trust to your so exercising your abilities and
improving the advantages of your past expensive
education, as soon to diminish *this* charge. I say
no more on that head.

Whatever you do, above all other things keep out
of debt and confide in me. If you ever find yourself on the verge of any perplexity or difficulty,

come to me. You will never find me hard with you while you are manly and truthful.

As your brothers have gone away one by one, I have written to each of them what I am now going to write to you. You know that you have never been hampered with religious forms of restraint, and that with mere unmeaning forms I have no sympathy. But I most strongly and affectionately impress upon you the priceless value of the New Testament, and the study of that book as the one unfailing guide in life. Deeply respecting it, and bowing down before the character of our Saviour, as separated from the vain constructions and inventions of men, you cannot go very wrong, and will always preserve at heart a true spirit of veneration and humility. Similarly I impress upon you the habit of saying a Christian prayer every night and morning. These things have stood by me all through my life, and remember that I tried to render the New Testament intelligible to you and lovable by you when you were a mere baby.

And so God bless you.

Ever your affectionate Father.

[TO MR. EDWARD BULWER LYTTON DICKENS][1]

My dearest Plorn :

I write this note to-day because your going away
is much upon my mind, and because I want you to
have a few parting words from me to think of now
and then at quiet times. I need not tell you that I
love you dearly, and am very, very sorry in my heart
to part with you. But this life is half made up of
partings, and these pains must be borne. It is my
comfort and my sincere conviction that you are going to try the life for which you are best fitted. I
think its freedom and wildness more suited to you
than any experiment in a study or office would ever
have been ; and without that training, you could
have followed no other suitable occupation.

What you have already wanted until now has
been a set, steady, constant purpose. I therefore
exhort you to persevere in a thorough determination to do whatever you have to do as well as you
can do it. I was not so old as you are now when I
first had to win my food, and do this out of this
determination, and I have never slackened in it
since.

Never take a mean advantage of anyone in any
transaction, and never be hard upon people who are

---

[1] Letter to his youngest son on his departure for Australia in 1868.

16

in your power. Try to do to others, as you would
have them do to you, and do not be discouraged if
they fail sometimes. It is much better for you that
they should fail in obeying the greatest rule laid
down by our Saviour, than that you should.

I put a New Testament among your books, for
the very same reasons, and with the very same hopes
that made me write an easy account of it for you,
when you were a little child. Because it is the best
book that ever was or will be known in the world,
and because it teaches you the best lessons by which
any human creature who tries to be truthful and
faithful to duty can possibly be guided. As your
brothers have gone away, one by one, I have written to each such words as I am now writing to you,
and have entreated them all to guide themselves by
this book, putting aside the interpretations and inventions of men.

You will remember that you have never at home
been wearied about religious observances or mere
formalities. I have always been anxious not to
weary my children with such things before they are
old enough to form opinions respecting them. You
will therefore understand the better that I now most
solemnly impress upon you the truth and beauty of
the Christian religion, as it came from Christ Himself, and the impossibility of your going far wrong
if you humbly but heartily respect it.

Only one thing more on this head. The more we are in earnest as to feeling it, the less we are disposed to hold forth about it. Never abandon the wholesome practice of saying your own private prayers, night and morning. I have never abandoned it myself, and I know the comfort of it.

I hope you will always be able to say in after life that you had a kind father. You cannot show your affection for him so well, or make him so happy, as by doing your duty.

Your affectionate Father.

Index.

INDEX.

Forster, John, 33, 35, and see Letters.
Franklin, Sir John, 97.

GAD'S HILL, Dickens's childish impressions of, 122.
Gallenga, 152.
Gaskell, Mrs., see Letters.
Great Expectations, letters concerning, 159, 161.
Grief, the perversity of, exemplified, 7.
Grisi, 95.

Hard Times, 96.,
Harness, Rev. W., see Letters.
Hillard, Mr., 36.
Hogarth, Miss, see Letters.
Holland House, 121.
Holmes, Mr. O. W., 199.
Hood, Tom, 84.
Household Words, 77, 80, 81, 92.
Hughes, Master Hastings, see Letters.
Hulkes, Mrs., 214.

ILLUSTRATIONS of Dickens's works, his descriptions for, 8, 9, 10.
Ireland, Alexander, see Letters.
Ireland, a dialogue in, 135-136; feeling for Dickens in, 138.
Irving, Washington, 227, and see Letters.
Italy, Dickens in, 47-52; in Venice, 47; at Naples, 89-91; Dickens on unity of, 159; his apology for Italians, 151.

JAMAICA, the insurrection in, 186.
Jerrold, Douglas, see Letters.
Jesuits' College, 152.

KNIGHT, Charles, see Letters.
Knowles, James Sheridan, 65.

LAMARTINE, 64.
Landor, Walter Savage, see Letters.
Lanman, Charles, see Letters.
Layard, A. H., see Letters.
Letters of Charles Dickens to :
Anonymous, 193.
Austin, Henry, 3, 27.
Boyle, Miss Mary, 71.
Cartwright, Samuel, 222.
Cattermole, George, 8, 10, 11.
Cerjat, M. de, 67, 98, 122, 145, 165, 170, 179, 186.
Chorley, Henry F., 150.
Collins, Wilkie, 86, 116, 118, 148, 175, 217.
Dickens, Charles, jr., 201.
Dickens, Mrs., 48, 53.
Dickens, Miss, 67, 137, 166, 198, 203, 205, 210, 212, 221, 225, 228.
Dickens, Henry F., 229, 238.
Dickens, Edward B. L., 241.
Eeles, Mr., 75.
Fechter, Mr. Charles, 232.
Felton, Prof., 31, 37, 39, 44.
Fields, James T., 195.
Finlay, F. D., 195.
Forster, John, 128, 141, 147, 153, 161.
Gaskell, Mrs., 77, 78.